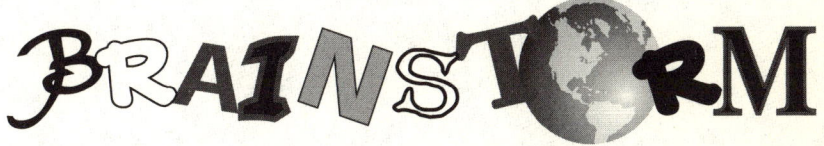

PIERCE FEIRTEAR

BLACKWATER PRESS

For Mark, Gavin and Darragh

© Copyright text: Pierce Feirtear

First published in 1997 by BLACKWATER PRESS, Unit 7/8, Broomhill Business Park, Dublin 24.

Printed at the press of the publishers.

All rights reserved. No part of this publication may be reproduced, stored in a retrieval system, or transmitted in any form, or by any means, electronic, mechanical, photocopying, recording, or otherwise, without the prior written permission of the publishers.

This book is subject to the conditions that it shall not, by way of trade or otherwise, be lent, resold, hired out or otherwise circulated without the publisher's prior consent in any form of binding or cover other than that in which it is published and without a similar condition being imposed on the subsequent purchaser.

ISBN: 0 86121 904 X

Editor: Deirdre Whelan
Assistant Editor: Zoë O'Connor
Design and Layout: Philip Ryan
Cover Art: Adrienne Geoghegan
Illustration: Marie-Louise Fitzpatrick, Aileen Caffrey, Kevin McSherry, Nicola Sedgwick

C·O·N·T·E·N·T·S

Brainstorm/Did You Know? 5
Believe it or Not! 6
Funny Money 7
A Rope Over Niagara 8
Party Fun 10
Wordsearch – The Big Screen 11
Jokes, Jokes, Jokes 12
Brainstorm/Did You Know? 14
Believe it or Not! 15
A Testing Time… 16
Magic Made Easy 18
A Riddle from Ancient Times 19
Jokes, Jokes, Jokes 20
Crossword – How Many? 22
Brainstorm/Did You Know? 23
Believe it or Not! 24
Wordsearch – Fashion Crazy 25
A Different Life 26
Simply Drawing 28
Famous Pairs 29
Jokes, Jokes, Jokes 30
Brainstorm/Did You Know? 32
Believe it or Not! 33
Great White Fright! 34
More Magic 36
More Tricks 37
Jokes, Jokes, Jokes 38
Crossword – Landmarks 40

Brainstorm/Did You Know? 41
Believe it or Not! 42
Nice Mice 43
Friend of the Elephants 44
Wordsearch – Sportsearch 46
Pop Puzzle 47
Jokes, Jokes, Jokes 48
Brainstorm/Did You Know? 50
Believe it or Not! 51
What's in an Orange? 52
Beat Your Drum 54
One-Handed Knot 55
Jokes, Jokes, Jokes 56
Crossword – Mixed Bag 58
Brainstorm/Did You Know? 59
Believe it or Not! 60
Meet Your Match 61
The Bug Man 62
Wordsearch – The Sound of Music 64
Track the Twister 65
Riddles from Old Ireland 66
Brainstorm/Did You Know? 68
Believe it or Not! 69
It Takes Courage! 70
Magic Numbers 72
King of the Jungle 73
Jokes, Joke, Jokes 74
Crossword – Americana 76

Brainstorm/Did You Know 77
Believe it or Not! 78
Brainteasers 79
Storm Clouds Over Everest 80
Wordsearch – Bananas! 82
Coin Magic 83
Jokes, Jokes, Jokes 84
Brainstorm/Did You Know? 86
Believe it or Not! 87
If it Glitters, it's Gold 88
Clowning Around 90
What's the Difference? 91
Jokes, Jokes, Jokes 92
Crossword – Hospital Health 94
Brainstorm/Did You Know? 95
Believe it or Not! 96
Puzzle it Out/Total Brainteaser 97
A Long Time Ago In a Galaxy Far, Far Away… 98
Jokes, Jokes, Jokes 100
Word Puzzle – The Right Order 102
Trick Your Friends 103
Make Your Own Ice Cream 104
Solutions **105**

BRAINSTORM

1. What is the longest snake in the world?
2. In which country would you spend escudos?
3. What is a young eel called?
4. Who invented the biro?
5. In which capital city are the Nobel Prizes awarded each year?
6. Who is buried in Graceland?
7. Where in the world would you take a lift on a gondola?
8. Who flies in the plane named *Airforce 1*?
9. What famous person was born in Mecca?
10. Name the computer that beat world champion Garry Kasparov at chess.

DID YOU KNOW?

The world's richest business person is Bill Gates, owner of Microsoft. Last year alone he earned $30 million a day.

The planet Pluto was only discovered in 1930.

The seahorse is a very special creature: it is the male seahorse, not the female, which gives birth to its young.

BELIEVE IT OR NOT!

Small is beautiful - at least that's what scientists working in micro-technology think. Nothing is too small for them. In Germany, they recently assembled a helicopter - the size of a wasp! It weighs less than half a gram, has two blades and, yes, it flies. In Japan, a working car no bigger than a grain of rice has been put together. One Japanese engineer at the University of Tokyo has even succeeded in creating an artificial insect that can fly (its wings are only 0.2mm wide). The tiny motors that power these devices can be used in a thousand different ways, and will transform our world, say the scientists.

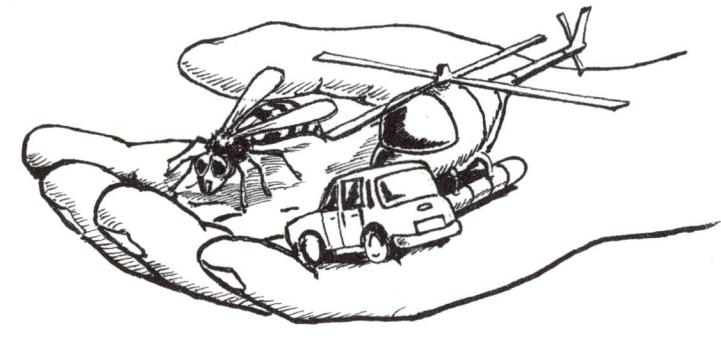

If you suspect there's an enemy spy in your organisation, one way to seek him or her out is to give lie-detector tests. Last year the American spy agency CIA ran this check on one of its senior agents, Harold J Nicholson. He failed, twice. A third test was given. One way of beating the lie-detector is to take a deep breath before you tell a lie. Just before answering the crucial questions, Nicholson was observed to be taking long deep breaths. He was told to stop. The question was put again. Nicholson failed the test again. He now faces charges of spying.

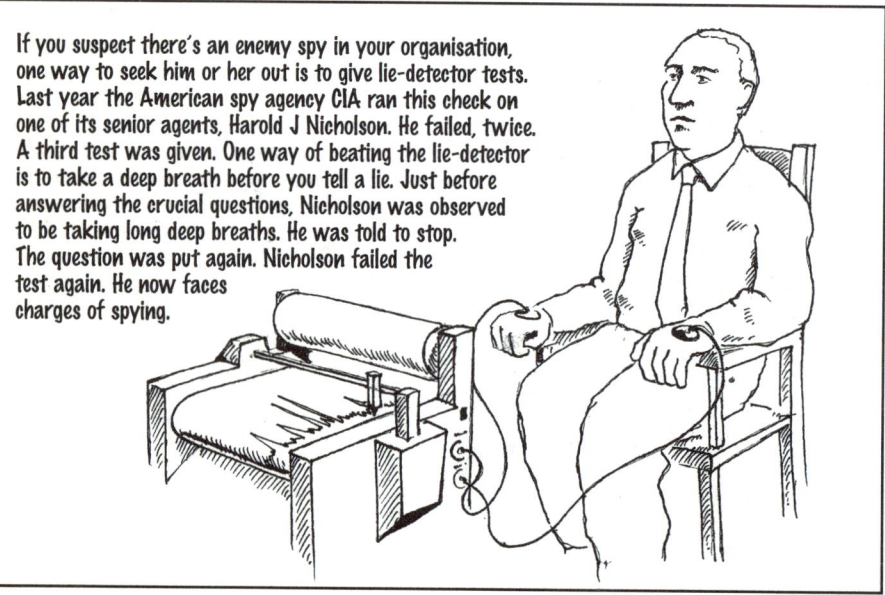

$ FUNNY MONEY $

Five Makes Seven

Place seven coins on a table as shown. One line of coins has five coins in it, while the other line has only three.
In just two moves, can you rearrange the coins so that there are an equal number of them in each line?

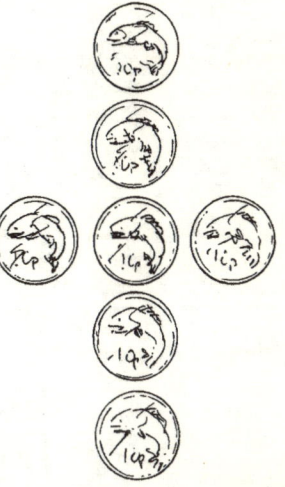

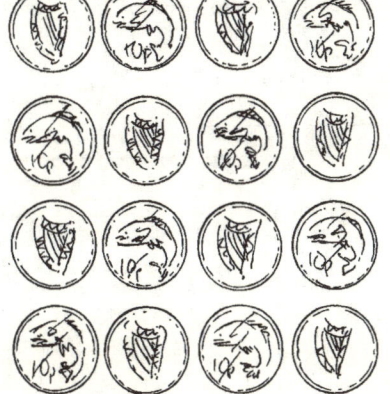

Harps and Fish

Lay out a square with sixteen 10p coins so that the harp and the fish are placed next to each other in each row as shown.

By making just two moves, can you rearrange the coins so that there are just harps in the first row, fish in the second row, harps in the third and fish in the fourth?

A Rope Over Niagara

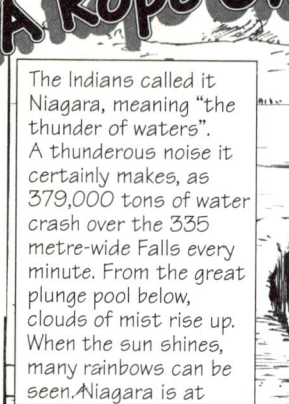

The Indians called it Niagara, meaning "the thunder of waters". A thunderous noise it certainly makes, as 379,000 tons of water crash over the 335 metre-wide Falls every minute. From the great plunge pool below, clouds of mist rise up. When the sun shines, many rainbows can be seen. Niagara is at once beautiful and terrifying.

In 1859, a Frenchman named Charles Blondin announced to the world that he was going to walk a tightrope across Niagara Falls. "Impossible," said the newspapers. "Too dangerous," advised his friends. But Mr Blondin could not be dissuaded.

He had begun his career as an acrobat, not a tightrope walker. Born near Calais in 1824, he was only 5 years old when he gave his first public performance – as "The Little Wonder". He soon moved on and up to the high wire, thrilling audiences all over Europe with his daredevil feats.

But at Niagara Falls in America he was to face the greatest challenge of his career... A huge crowd had gathered for the event. The great rope – 49 metres above the raging waters – was stretched across from one side to the other.
A hush fell over the crowd as Blondin stepped on to it. Eyes fixed straight ahead, he moved very slowly at first, making his way out over the roaring abyss. Growing in confidence, he picked up speed. After ten minutes, he was halfway across.

Then he stopped. He lowered a rope down to a ship waiting below in case of an accident. He was about to abandon the attempt, it seemed.

But out there, in the middle, the wind was blowing hard. The rope began to sag and sway. Spectators gasped as Blondin was seen to falter and almost lose balance.

Then, to everyone's astonishment, a sailor on deck tied a bottle to the rope and Blondin hauled it up.

The daring Frenchman then poured out a drink for himself and, standing on one leg, raised his glass to the crowd and drank their health! Ten minutes later, he was home and dry...

That was only the first of several times that Charles Blondin walked across Niagara Falls. He walked across it with his feet in a sack...

He walked it on stilts...

He walked it blindfold.

On one occasion he even walked it with a man on his back...

On another, he took a man across in a wheelbarrow.

Blondin will always be remembered as king of the tightrope.

PARTY FUN

1. The Balloon That Does Not Burst

Next time you have a party, amaze your friends with this trick. You will need two balloons. Blow up the first balloon. Stick a pin in it. What happens? The balloon bursts with a bang. Now you blow up the second balloon. This balloon has a piece of cellotape stuck on it (which you put on earlier). Stick a pin through the cellotape and… the balloon won't burst!

2. The Flying Coin Trick

For this trick you will need two wine glasses. Put a 2p coin in one of the glasses. Turn to your friends and say: "Now, I am going to pass the coin from one glass to the other without touching it." "You must be joking, let's see you try!" they will answer. All you have to do then is simply blow down on to the coin. It will spin around the glass and – with a bit of practice – will pop out into the other glass!

THE BIG SCREEN

The names of 20 top movies are hidden here. How many can you find?

```
O S M L E M P E R T E R E M U I M P
W U A T E F L O N D W I N I N N I E
E P R B R A V E H E A R T C U D C E
R E I B A L P A T E T M I H E E H O
E R R P I T S T A L E W R A T P E N
T M H A F N M I D C R E L E P E R T
W A R L O L J A W S W I F L P N O P
O N R A D I D O N P O N E C E D B I
V X Z D N O T A F E R I T O L E E N
S U P D R S A T Y E L N B L G N T O
R O B I N H O O D L D D A L E C I C
S K O N M A L M I D I E T I J E H C
P E R A N S T A M A N G M N E D O H
A T S J G H O R S T I R H S R A V I
T E W O E S P A C E J A M T R Y P O
E R U I G R G L X W I M A O O N I W
R L P U N J U A E T R E T P G A R A
M I R I T S N D U P N V I S H W E T
A P U N D E R S I E G E L U O R A E
M P I B H X Q V R W Z U D T S Q S P
E S T A R W A R S U E R A T T P W K
J E R R Y M A G U I R E K C Z B J L
```

JOKES JOKES JOKES

What would you call a laughing motorbike?
A Yamaha ha!

What did the river say when the elephant sat in it?
Well, I'll be damned.

What do you get if you cross a skunk and a boomerang?
A bad smell you can't get rid of.

Teacher: Anna, if you had 15 cows and you bought 27 more cows at the market, what would you have?
Anna: A dairy herd.

What happens when the price of pork goes up?
Pigs fly.

Why did 5 eat 6?
Because 7 8 9.

What would you call a healthy Spaniard?
Manuel.

What happened when the carrot died?
There was a great turnip at the funeral.

Teacher: Niamh, who was the first woman in the world?
Niamh: Can I have a hint, Miss?
Teacher: Yes, think of an apple.
Niamh: The first woman was Granny Smith!

Did you hear about the duck who became a cowboy?
He was quack on the draw.

Why are elephants so poor?
Because they work for peanuts.

BRAINSTORM

1. Which movie hero lives in Gotham City?
2. What drink did Dom Peter Perignon invent?
3. Where in the world is the Golden Gate Bridge?
4. Who painted the Mona Lisa?
5. The month of August is named after which person?
6. In golf, what is two shots below par called?
7. What does a toxicologist study?
8. Who was Adi Dassler?
9. How many sides has a decagon?
10. Name the girl who went to the Mad Hatter's tea party.

DID YOU KNOW?

Gay Byrne's 35-year-old Late Late Show on RTÉ is the longest running chat show in the world.

English author Barbara Cartland, aged 95, has so far written 637 books.

In 1960 a seven-year-old boy was swept over Niagara Falls and rescued unharmed.

BELIEVE IT OR NOT!

One winter a young American businessman went to the frozen north of Canada to buy furs. Fresh food was hard to find there, but the local people had a solution – they ate food which they had previously frozen. Fascinated by this, the American returned to New York and began to experiment.

His aim was to try and find the best way of freezing food without losing the flavour. In 1925, he became the first person to sell frozen foods on the market. His business grew and grew. His name: Clarence Birdseye.

It's not just spiders and snakes you need to watch out for in Australia but also... magpies. A recent survey has shown that a staggering 95% of men and 75% of women had at one time been attacked by the birds. Most had been attacked as children and a quarter of them had needed medical attention. Magpies become nasty during the mating season and will attack if they feel their chicks are threatened. Their favourite targets are young boys, cyclists and joggers. The report adds that there is also a small number of "looney birds" which attack people all year round!

A Testing Time...

The speed of sound is known as Mach 1. This speed can vary from 660 mph to 760 mph depending on temperature, altitude and windspeed. When World War 2 ended, there was a race to build an aircraft that could match such a speed. The Americans had a secret airfield called Muroc in the Mojave Desert in California. Here, in 1947, they began testing the X-1, a bullet-shaped aircraft with four rocket chambers. They were pinning their hopes on the X-1. But they needed the right pilot.

In stepped Chuck Yeager, a daring airforce pilot. He had been a fighter pilot in the war. He knew the risks involved in these tests.

The day chosen for the big test was Tuesday, October 14th. On the Sunday before it, he took his horse for a ride into the desert. His wife Glennis went with him. Night was falling as they returned. It would be fun, they thought, to race back to the stables... As Chuck galloped into the corral, his horse banged into a gate and he was thrown to the ground. He knew from the piercing pain that his ribs were broken.

If he told the doctors, the test would be cancelled – or even worse, another pilot might take his place. He decided to say nothing. But by Tuesday the pain was so bad he could not raise his right arm. He needed that right arm to pull shut the hatch of the X-1 cockpit...

Arriving at Muroc, he went straight to his friend, flight engineer Jack Ridley. Jack had a solution. He made a device out of a broomstick for closing the hatch. And when no one was about, Jack hid it in the cockpit.

Now, the X-1 had only enough fuel for three minutes of flight, so it had to be strapped under the belly of a B-29 bomber and carried 9,000 metres into the air before the flight could be attempted.

The B-29 took off. At 2,000 metres, Chuck climbed down a ladder into the X-1 cockpit. Using the broomstick, he managed to shut the hatch. He was ready.

At 9,000 metres the B-29 let go of its load.

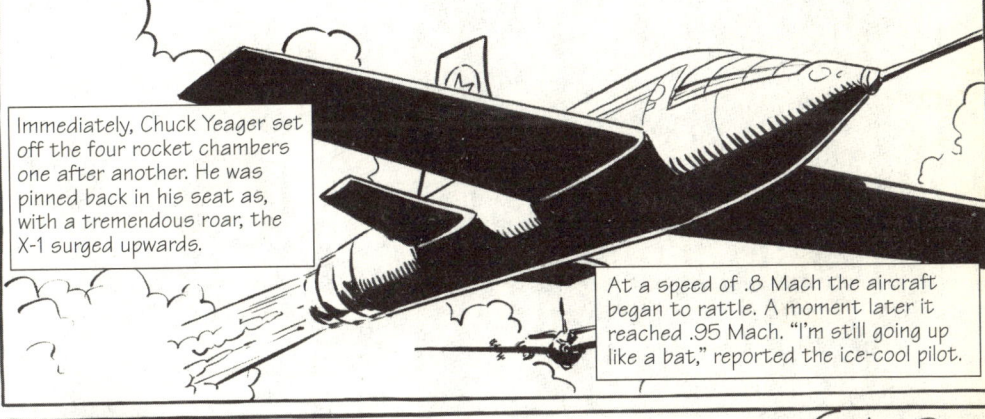

Immediately, Chuck Yeager set off the four rocket chambers one after another. He was pinned back in his seat as, with a tremendous roar, the X-1 surged upwards.

At a speed of .8 Mach the aircraft began to rattle. A moment later it reached .95 Mach. "I'm still going up like a bat," reported the ice-cool pilot.

Then the people on the ground heard a loud BOOM! as the X-1 went supersonic at 1.05 Mach. The sound barrier had been broken.

MAGIC MADE EASY

In this book you will discover some great tricks to try out on your friends, but you should remember two golden rules:

First, "practice makes perfect" – keep practising the trick till you get it right.

Second, only do the trick once. If you do it a second or a third time, your friends might discover how you do it.

Here's an excellent magic trick to begin with:

Pennies from Heaven
You will place five coins on a table, scoop them up into your empty hands, then open your hands again to show seven coins! (All you need is seven coins and a piece of Blu-Tack!) Before your friends come into the room, use the Blu-Tack to stick two of the coins under the table. When your friends come in, show them the five coins and place them in a row at the edge of the table. Show your empty hands to your audience. Place your left hand close to the edge of the table, near the hidden coins. Use your right hand to brush the five coins off the table into your left hand. Your friends will be watching the five coins and won't notice your left hand reaching below the table to pull off the other two coins.
Shake the coins in your hands, say the magic word ABRACADABRA and drop the seven coins on to the table...

A Riddle from Ancient Times

Once upon a time a rich merchant set out for the great bazaar of Baghdad. He carried with him three balls of solid gold which he hoped to sell for a vast sum of money. Each of the golden balls weighed 1 kilogram. On the way he came to a bridge which he had to cross. He stopped, for there was a problem. The problem was, the bridge could only support a weight of 100 kilograms – and he weighed 99 kilograms, without the golden balls. To make matters worse, the bridge sloped upwards, was 400 metres wide, and he was only allowed cross it once. How would he get his gold safely across?

JOKES JOKES JOKES

Why did the cows huddle together in the rain?
To keep each udder dry.

Dad: I've made the chicken soup.
Daughter: But I thought you were making the soup for us.

What do you get if you cross a Brontosaurus with a cow?
A lot of milk.

What did the priest say when he saw insects on his roses?
Let us spray.

How does a monkey make toast?
He puts it under the gorilla.

HOW MANY?

ACROSS

2. Commandments in the Bible.
4. Players on a gaelic football team.
7. Counties in Ulster.
9. Players on a soccer team.
10. Days in April.
13. How many players are needed to play the card game "patience"?
14. Days in a fortnight.

DOWN

1. How many days in the Christmas season?
2. How many in a score?
3. How many musketeers?
5. How many in a baker's dozen?
6. There are a _ _ _ _ _ _ _ years in a century.
8. Characters in Enid Blyton's "Famous _ _ _ _" stories.
11. How many in a pair of anything?
12. The number of seasons in each year.

BRAINSTORM

1. How many stars are there on the US flag?
2. Which islands were named after King Philip of Spain?
3. What is Britain's only poisonous snake called?
4. How does a blind person know when he or she is handling a £10 note?
5. What is a comet made of?
6. Which type of road surface did John MacAdam invent?
7. What do the actors Pierce Brosnan and Sean Connery have in common?
8. What number does the Roman numeral C stand for?
9. What nickname do Americans have for a tornado?
10. Who won gold for Ireland in the 1992 Olympics?

DID YOU KNOW?

The word NIKE means "victory" – after the Greek goddess of victory.

America's most experienced astronaut is Shannon Lucid. She spent 235 days in orbit.

All the pet hamsters in the world are descended from a single female and her litter of 12 young, discovered in Syria in 1930.

BELIEVE IT OR NOT!

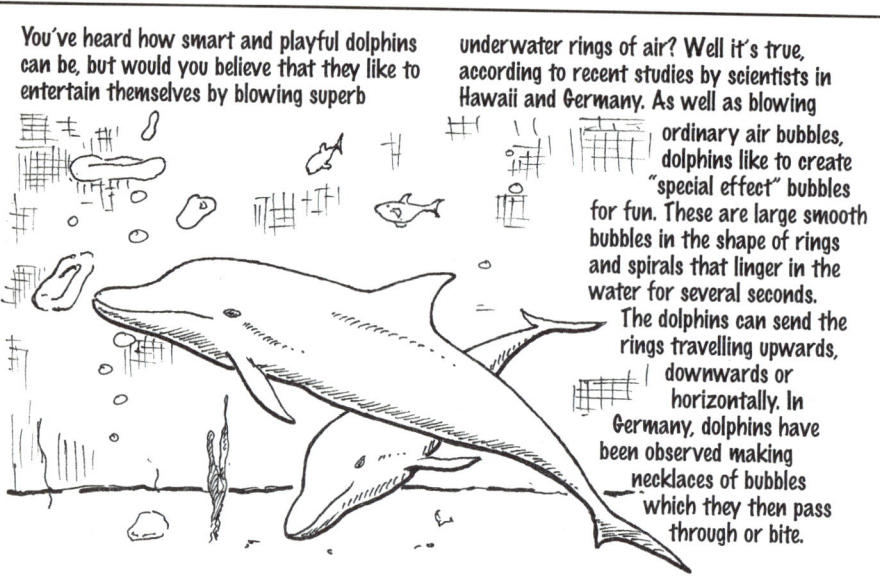

You've heard how smart and playful dolphins can be, but would you believe that they like to entertain themselves by blowing superb underwater rings of air? Well it's true, according to recent studies by scientists in Hawaii and Germany. As well as blowing ordinary air bubbles, dolphins like to create "special effect" bubbles for fun. These are large smooth bubbles in the shape of rings and spirals that linger in the water for several seconds. The dolphins can send the rings travelling upwards, downwards or horizontally. In Germany, dolphins have been observed making necklaces of bubbles which they then pass through or bite.

One of the world's great unsolved mysteries concerns the whereabouts of the famed Amber Room, once known as the "Eighth Wonder of the World". Amber is formed from fossilised tree sap and, in 1755, one entire room of the Catherine Palace at St Petersburg in Russia was adorned with this semi-precious gem. Almost 100,000 amber pieces were carved into flowers and royal emblems and mounted on panels covering 55 square metres. In September 1939 this $100 million treasure fell into the hands of the invading German army. By the end of World War 2 it had vanished.

FASHION CRAZY

We've hidden the names of 20 items of clothing and footwear in this wordsearch. Also hidden are the names of 5 of the world's top clothes and sportswear companies. That's 25 words in all – but can you search them out? The names read across, down and diagonally.

```
C A P K L E V I S P J E A N S W
H R T Q O J A C K E T O V C O L
R Z Y D H P Q Z X R K B H G C M
U E S A R U V N X T I E O W K L
N X B E A E V B P Q R N V P S Z
N H J Q A Z S H Z Q R E G J P W
E D Z E T E E S H I R T H K O P
R G N C R Q Z X C V B T R P K J
S F V B A S Y Q B S H O E S N V
J W T I C M E G V N O N A Z X F
W C G B K W R Y H P L P M K Z X
D J U R S H O R T S L M O I E S
V Z S S U P W F V J X C O A T N
X B A D I D A S M L I Q P I D I
B G N V T H W A S C B M I U Y T
M L H E W S W E A T S H I R T C
S D O N M P Q E T D A F Z C V X
D G H U H W S O C A R D I G A N
B G J K S A N D A L S O T Y K I
N O F V W E G M X C V R E L A K
J K O G J W R T Y U I S D F G E
B M Z T R O U S E R S H Q E X Z
A F D I S H Q A S D E R F T V N
A R E E B O K J I G L O V E S Z
```

A Different Life!

When her husband died in 1915, Marguerite Baker Harrison was left penniless. Anxious to find work, she decided to try her hand as a reporter. Though she had no experience, her local newspaper, the Baltimore Sun, gave her a job. Soon she was writing articles about fashion shows and tea parties. Quickly she grew bored.

Marguerite wanted a more exciting life... she wanted to be a spy! World War 1 was drawing to a close, so there was no time to lose. "I speak fluent French and German and have a good accent in Italian…

…Without any trouble I could pass as a French woman and, after a little practice, as a Swiss-German," she wrote to the spy division of the US War Department.

She got the job. But by the time she reached Germany, the war had ended.

So in 1920 she was sent to Russia. This was a dangerous mission. Communists had taken control of the government there. The secret police were everywhere. Thousands of citizens had been arrested.

Maguerite spent months undercover in Moscow smuggling out information.

Finally, the secret police caught up with her and she was thrown into the infamous Lubianka Prison. As Prisoner Number 2961, she endured almost a year of hardship and misery.

After her release, she returned to the US. Her cover blown, she could no longer work as a spy. Instead Marguerite wanted to travel and write. So in 1922 she set out on a trip to Asia. Crossing the Pacific by ship, she landed in Japan.

Next she travelled to Korea, and from there into China. Her plan now was to turn back. But Marguerite wasn't one for sticking to plans.

Instead of backtracking, she decided to push on all the way across Asia into Europe. "Well, it seemed like a good idea at the time!" she said afterwards. So she drove her car across the Gobi Desert in Mongolia.

Then she headed into Siberia, part of Russia. Here she was arrested, accused again of being a spy, and brought by train to Moscow.

Marguerite had been given a valid visa to visit Russia and she was furious. After two months the secret police set her free.

Her next move was into film-making. She travelled to Persia where she filmed a tribe of nomads migrating with their flocks over the Zagros Mountains. The 48-day trek was difficult and dangerous.

No outsiders had ever explored these mountain passes before. Released in 1925, the movie "Grass" was one of the first ever documentaries to be made.

SIMPLY DRAWING

Use the grid to copy this picture.

FAMOUS PAIRS

What name will complete these famous pairs?

Fred Flintstone and Barney rubble
Tom and ......!
Batman and robin
Cain and able
Lois Lane and superman
Adam and eve
Zig and zag
Jack and the bean stalk
Romulus and Rumulus
Marks and menser
Samson and lion
Beavis and Buthead
Anthony and ?
Hansel and gretal
Laurel and hardey
David and goliath
Tweedledum and tweedledee
Jeckyll and hyde

And now for some harder ones

Neil Armstrong and ....
Edmund Hillary and ....
Alan Hale and ....
Gottlieb Daimler and ....
John Alcock and ....
David Livingstone and ....

JOKES JOKES JOKES

What do you call a zebra with no stripes?
A horse.

Why was the Egyptian girl confused?
Because her daddy was a mummy.

What do you get if you cross a motorway with a skateboard?
Run over.

Teacher: John, put the word "centimetre" in a sentence for us.
John: My aunty flew in from America and my dad was centimetre.

Why did the golfer change her shoes?
Because she got a hole in one.

How do you hire a horse?
Stand it on a platform.

How do you catch a squirrel?
Climb up a tree and act like a nut.

Mum: Be a good boy and tell me if the indicator lights are working.
Son: Yes, no, yes, no, yes, no, yes, no…

John: Teacher, do you think it's fair to punish someone for something they didn't do?
Teacher: Most definitely not.
John: That's a relief – I didn't do my homework.

What do you get if you cross a bear with a skunk?
Winnie the Pooh.

How do you make antifreeze?
Send her to Antarctica.

31

BRAINSTORM

1. What did Neil Armstrong say as he stepped on to the Moon?
2. How many strings are there on a guitar?
3. Tirana is the capital of which European country?
4. Give another name for your skull.
5. In which South American country did the Indians known as the Aztecs live?
6. If you kiss the Blarney Stone in Cork, what gift are you said to receive?
7. What is a supernova?
8. Which ship, built in Belfast, hit an iceberg and sank on its maiden voyage?
9. Name an indoor sport played with 22 balls.
10. Which Irish Nobel Prize winner is featured on the £20 note?

DID YOU KNOW?

The mountain called Mauna Kea forms one of the Hawaiian islands. From the floor of the sea to the top, it measures 10,203 metres, almost 1,500 metres taller than Mount Everest.

The world's first duty free shop opened in Shannon Airport in 1951.

Doberman dogs are named after the German tax collector, Ludwig Dobermann, who bred them as his personal guard dogs.

BELIEVE IT OR NOT!

Instead of hauling tree trunks around for a living, one clever Indian elephant has switched to washing cars - at $500 a time. Judy is a 4-ton, 31-year-old Indian elephant and the star attraction at the Marine World Africa animal park in Vallejo, California, USA. She begins by filling her trunk with 8 gallons of water from a bucket - at one go - and then lets fly with a high pressure squirt all over the car. Next she sponges it down. After that, she dries it off with a towel. For the final touch, she vacuums the car with her trunk!

British scientists in Antarctica have recently discovered a huge freshwater lake there. The lake is locked between layers of ice four kilometres below the surface. The lake, christened Lake Vostok, is the size of Munster and is 100 metres deep. The four-kilometre layer of packed ice on top of it creates such great pressure that the lake is kept liquid in the below-zero temperatures. There might even be living organisms in the lake, say the scientists.

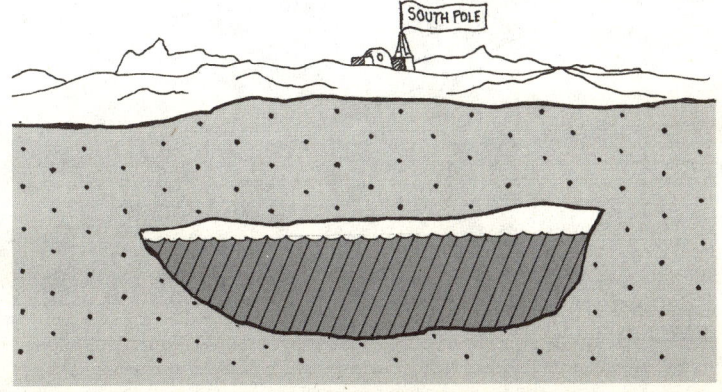

Great White Fright!

The most fearsome of all sharks is the Great White. This deadly predator can detect one part of blood in 10 million parts of water.

Coming in for the attack at a t speed of 25 mph, its black eyes roll back into the sockets, and great jaws open wide revealing f rows of razor-sharp teeth.

Thankfully, it dislikes cold waters and you will not find the Great White anywhere near Ireland's shores!

But if you live in the tropical or subtropical regions it's a different matter. Each year between 70 – 100 people are attacked by sharks.

Divers and surfers who venture out to deeper waters are most at risk.

But even in-shore it's not safe. Many beaches around the world today have to be cordoned off by anti-shark nets to protect bathers.

Valerie Taylor, an Australian, knows all there is to know about t Great White. She and her husband Ron have filmed them over number of years. The documentary they made in 1994, "Blue Waters, White Death" is regarded as one of the best nature fil of all time. Naturally, all the underwater filming is done from inside heavily protected shark cages.

Two years ago Valerie was contacted by the Natal Sharks Board in South Africa, one of the world's top shark research centres. They had developed a new anti-shark device for protecting divers. Would she and Ron care to try it out?

The Natal Sharks Board had designed an "anti-shark" 90-volt power pack that could be fitted on to a scuba diver's back. A cable ran down from the pack to the diver's flippers. When the power pack was switched on, it generated a 7-metre-wide electrical field around the swimmer.

The field was too weak to be detected by humans, but as for the sharks — they hated it!

Valerie and Ron agreed to test the device. They went to Milne Bay in Papua New Guinea, where they threw buckets of meat overboard. Within minutes, sharks arrived and a feeding frenzy broke out.

Then Valerie and Ron put on their power packs and swam in among them — without shark cages! Immediately, the sharks fled, leaving the food behind. In March 1997, the couple tried out the device again, this time on the Great White. It worked. Even the Great White took fright.

MORE MAGIC

The Magic Glass
This is one of the oldest and best magic tricks.
All you need is a coin, a glass and a sheet of newspaper.
1. Sit at the top of the table (ask your friends to sit at the sides). Place a coin on the table. Tell your friends that, by using magical powers, you will make the coin go right through the table.
2. Wrap the sheet of newspaper tightly around the glass, making sure that none of the glass is sticking out at the bottom. Picking up the glass, place it over the coin and say the magic words "ABRACADABRA..."

3. When you lift the glass, show surprise that the coin is still there. So, with a wave of your hands place the glass back down over the coin and say the magic words a second time... Once more you lift the glass and the coin is there. You pull the glass back to the edge of the table and stare in amazement at the coin...
4. Tell your friends that you will try it one more time. While their eyes are fixed on the coin, you let the glass slip out of the newspaper and into your lap.
5. The newspaper looks as if the glass is still beneath it, so – for the third time – you bring it down over the coin. As you do so, say the magical words louder than ever and slap the paper down on to the coin and table top! Lifting the paper, you tell your friends that the magic was so strong, the glass went through the table instead of the coin... you reach under the table and bring out the glass for all to see!
Your friends will probably ask you to do the Magic Glass trick again. You should only do it once, however. Here's another trick to keep them happy...

MORE TRICKS

The Scratcher
Make sure there's a tablecloth on the table before doing this trick. Place a 5p coin on the table. Place a glass down over the coin but resting on two 20p coins. Because the glass is resting on the 20p coins, there is enough of a gap for the 5p coin to slide underneath... But the problem is: how do you get the 5p coin out from underneath the glass without touching it or the glass or the 20p coins? Your friends will scratch their heads... but all you have to do is scratch the tablecloth away from the glass and the coins slips out!

JOKES JOKES JOKES

What did Neptune say when the sea ran dry?
I haven't a notion!

Knock, knock!
Who's there?
Cook.
Cook who?
It must be spring, the bird's are singing again.

Knock, knock!
Who's there?
Irish stew.
Irish stew who?
Irish stew in the name of the law!

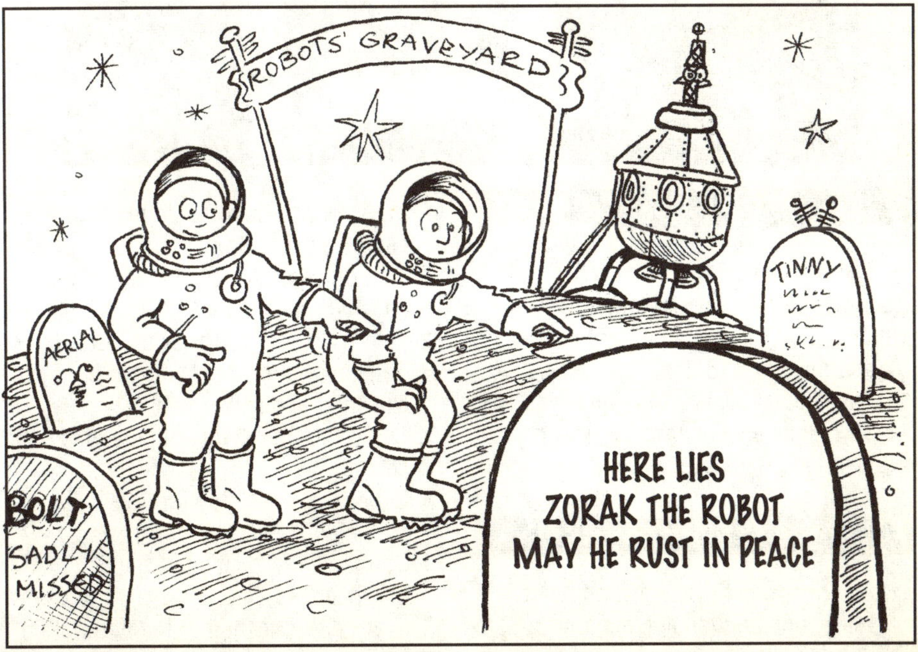

LANDMARKS

ACROSS

6. Tomb of queen located in India.
8. Name of this famous Paris tower.
10. Once the tallest building in New York and the world (6, 5).
13. The highest peak in the Himalayas.
14. This clock tower can be seen and heard in London (3, 3).

DOWN

1. American west coast city, home of Hollywood and many filmstars (3, 7).
2. Partly ruined open air amphitheatre can be seen in Rome.
3. This Chinese wall can be seen from space (5, 4).
4. The _ _ _ _ _ _ _ Tower of Pisa.
5. The London palace, home to the Queen of England.
7. City where the Statue of Liberty can be seen (3, 4).
9. Country in which to view the pyramids.
11. German city. Location of the Brandenburg Gate.
12. Greek city. Location of the Acropolis.

BRAINSTORM

1. What do the letters SAE stand for?
2. Which country is called Nippon by its people?
3. Where in your body is your larynx?
4. How many players are there on a basketball team?
5. What is the national anthem of the USA?
6. What is the difference between a dromedary camel and a bactrian camel?
7. Which car was named after the car manufacturer's daughter?
8. What date does St Valentine's Day fall on?
9. Name the queen of Egypt who is said to have died of a snake bite.
10. What is a Portuguese man-o'-war?

DID YOU KNOW?

The *Saturn 5* rocket which propelled American astronauts to the Moon stood as tall as a 36-storey skyscraper.

Saint Valentine is buried in Dublin. His bones lie under the altar of Whitefriars Church, Aungier Street.

The youngest person to sail around the world alone is 18-year old Australian David Dicks. He completed his 21,740-mile non-stop voyage in November 1996, after 264 days at sea.

BELIEVE IT OR NOT!

The Colosseum, built in AD 80, was the largest outdoor arena in ancient Rome. It had over 80 entrances and could accommodate 50,000 spectators. On hot summer days huge canvas awnings (shelters) were lowered over the terraces to provide shade from the sun. As well as gladiator fights, mock naval battles were staged there.

These sea battles were spectacular affairs. The whole arena was flooded with water and full-sized galleys rowed in to complete the effect. The emperor once held a great candle-lit dinner party in the Colosseum for 60,000 guests!

The world's smallest violin is 37 millimetres long and small enough to fit into a matchbox. But, for its maker, Manuel Ussa of Spain, it is one of his bigger pieces as most of his art-work can only be seen with the aid of a microscope! These works include: statues of Adam and Eve carved on the head of a pencil, the Tower Bridge of London set in the eye of a needle, and a pair of birds tending a nest of three eggs on the tip of a hair. Ussa's microscopic art can be viewed – under microscope – in a museum in Jersey, Channel Islands.

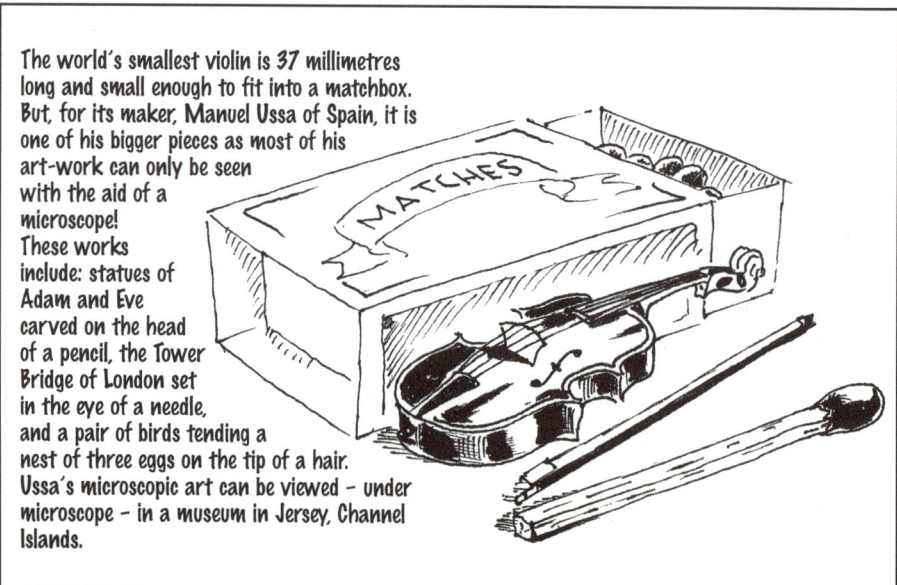

NICE MICE

Like to make some mice sweets? It's easy. Here's how:
All you need are the following ingredients:

1 egg
100g icing sugar
peppermint essence
(just a few drops)

pink food colouring
(just a few drops)
a few licorice strings
some currants and almond nuts

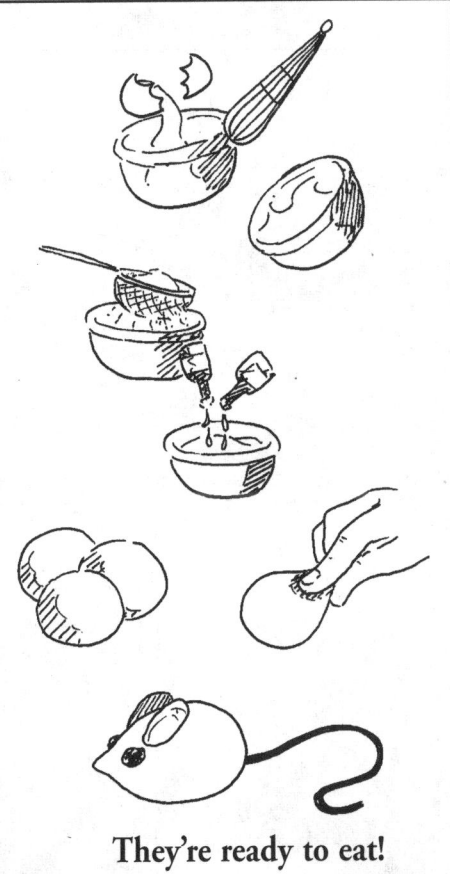

1. Separate the white of the egg from the egg yolk (the yellow part). Put the white of the egg in a bowl and beat it until it turns frothy.
2. Put the icing sugar through a sieve into another bowl. Then mix in the white of egg and stir it around well.
3. Add three or four drops of the peppermint essence and use your hands to mix it right through the mixture.
4. Add three or four drops of the pink food colouring and knead it into the mixture also.
5. Divide the pink mixture into six equal parts. Make each one into a round shape, like a mouse. Remember to pinch one end to make the mouse's snout!
6. Put two currants for the eyes, two almonds for the ears, and a piece of licorice string for the tail.

They're ready to eat!

Friend of the Elephants

Parbati Barua knows more about the Asian elephant than just about anyone else. She should know. She was born in an elephant camp. She grew up among them. Her father, Laljee Barua, was the most famous elephant handler in all of India.

As a child, she loved to go and sit among the elephants. There was a blind elephant she particularly loved. She sang to it all day, talked to it, looked after it. But the day came when she had to leave the camp to attend school.

She was away for six months. On the day she returned, she went first to her favourite elephant. Saying not a word, she sat a little away among all the other handlers. The elephant recognised her at once and threw a small stick into her lap.

At the age of 16, she set out to capture her first wild elephant. She searched through the jungle till she came upon a herd. Climbing on to a trained elephant, she selected one of the smaller wild ones, and moved towards it.

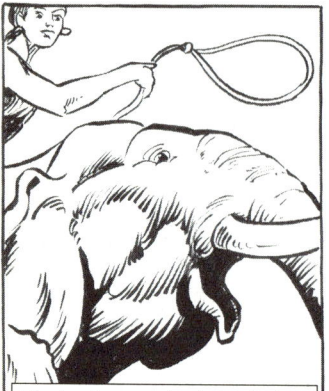

Elephants are shortsighted and Parbati was able to sneak up close to it. But how to lasso it?

Now, besides being shortsighted, an elephant has one other weakness. Its trunk is its most prized possession, and the moment it senses danger it tucks it into its mouth.

No sooner had Parbati thrown the noose over its head than the elephant did exactly that, and the rope slid into place.

Today, many years later, Parbati still travels everywhere on Lakhi, the elephant she lasooed and trained.

At one time there were millions of elephants in Asia. Now only 50,000 remain, nearly all of them in India. And the wild herds in India are under threat. The forests where they roam are dwindling fast as people clear the land for farming or chop down trees for firewood.

As a result, hungry elephants stray into the big tea plantations searching for food. Once this happens, there is trouble. People have been trampled. Elephants have been shot.

"We must protect the elephants, like jewels."

Nowadays, Parbati spends much of her time trying to keep the herds clear of the plantations. She often has to tend wounded elephants. She mixes ancient medicines in a bowl and always sings to calm the frightened animal. She is deeply concerned about the plight of these majestic creatures.

SPORTSEARCH

The names of 20 sports are to be found here. They read across, down and diagonally.

```
G H R I N G X O B H K H O K E P F O
O U O T A B R R A O K L D A F O E S
R R G C Y C L I N G R C A R A R N Q
L K B K K U R E D T A S C A R I P U
F I Y T R E L M N E N T E T B E S A
T B O S F I Y G E L T S T E Y N G S
S U R F I N G E N R E W U Y O T N H
O U B O I X N E T O R I B B X E I B
C F R T E N N I S U R M F O N E N O
K R A T F J U N O S W M F W I R G W
E A P L O T O G E K P I S L N I T L
Q R T F E N C S N I G N L I E N R E
T C D A L K B O X I N G R N Y G L N
E H O L T E R C G N I N O G E L O T
F E N C I N G C Y G O F I L G R L E
N R A R T O K E C H O K C E F Y I F
A Y S T Y W M R L E T L Z C X C I F
S A S H E R J U O K H U R L I N G I
J R T N I S N M O E K N J U D O T S
O B A D M I N T O N E N U D G E L Y
R Q G Y M N A S T I C S D N O B E R
L N G I B A N S K R W P I Y G B Y U
```

46

POP PUZZLE

How many top pop stars can you unscramble on the guitar and drums?

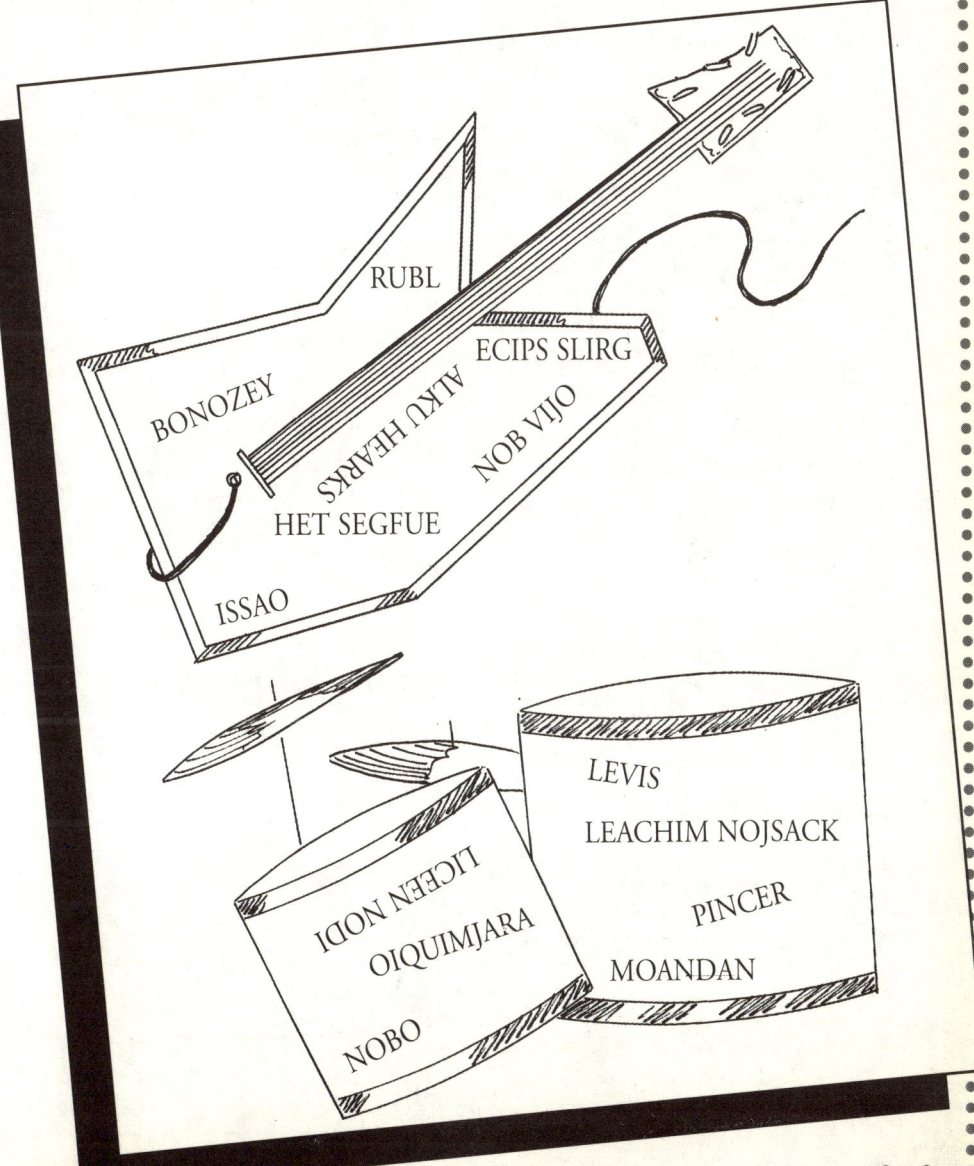

JOKES JOKES JOKES

Did you hear about the cross-eyed teacher?
She couldn't control her pupils.

Why are there no aspirins in the jungle?
Because the paracetamol.

Why did the skeleton not cross the road?
Because it didn't have the guts.

What did the baby chicken say when its mother laid an orange?
Look what Mama laid!

Doctor, Doctor, I think I'm a goat. How long have you been thinking this?
Ever since I was a kid.

What did the pin say to the balloon?
Come here or I'll burst you.

What happens to a duck before it grows up?
It grows down.

Doctor, Doctor, I feel like a bridge.
What's come over you?
A car, a truck and a lorry!

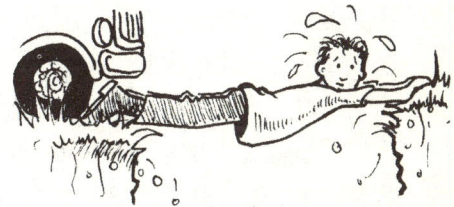

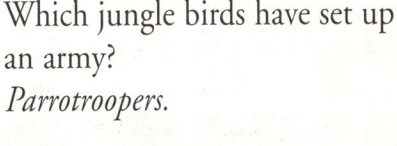

Which jungle birds have set up an army?
Parrotroopers.

What do you call a cowboy in debt?
The Loan Ranger.

BRAINSTORM

1. Which 21-year-old won the US Masters Golf Championship in 1997?
2. Name the only animal with four knees.
3. If you suffered from arachnophobia, what would you be very frightened of?
4. What is the least populated country in the world?
5. Name the only metal which is liquid at ordinary temperature.
6. Which one of these countries has a border with Russia: Norway, Sweden, Denmark?
7. What did Thomas Edison invent in 1879?
8. From which animal is the meat known as venison obtained?
9. Who directed the movies *E.T.*, *Jaws*, and *Jurassic Park*?
10. What is the Koran?

DID YOU KNOW?

Every zebra has a unique pattern of stripes, in the same way as each human has a unique pattern of fingerprints.

Around 5 cms of snow falls each year in the coldest Arctic regions – this is only slightly more than falls on the Sahara Desert.

The term "checkmate" in chess comes from the Persian "shah mat" meaning "the king is dead".

BELIEVE IT OR NOT!

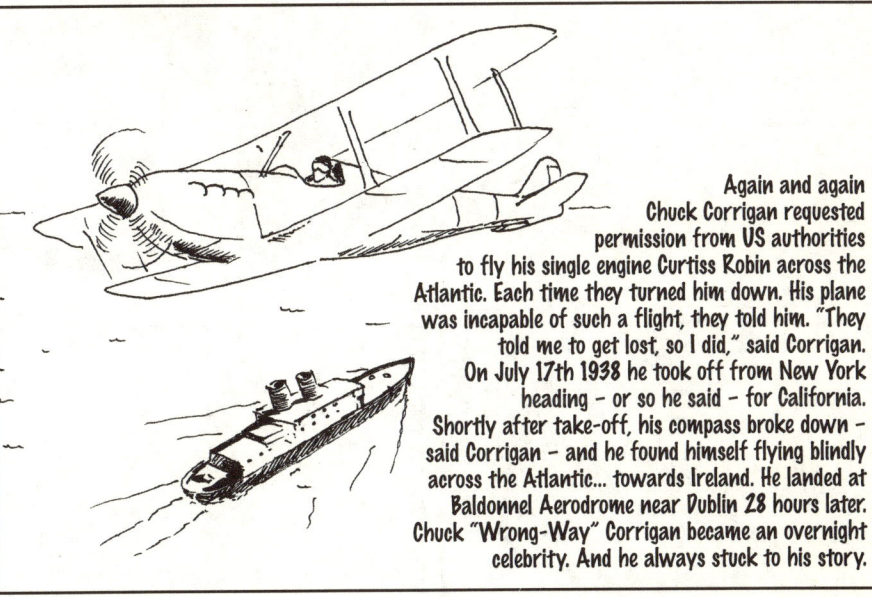

Again and again Chuck Corrigan requested permission from US authorities to fly his single engine Curtiss Robin across the Atlantic. Each time they turned him down. His plane was incapable of such a flight, they told him. "They told me to get lost, so I did," said Corrigan. On July 17th 1938 he took off from New York heading – or so he said – for California. Shortly after take-off, his compass broke down – said Corrigan – and he found himself flying blindly across the Atlantic... towards Ireland. He landed at Baldonnel Aerodrome near Dublin 28 hours later. Chuck "Wrong-Way" Corrigan became an overnight celebrity. And he always stuck to his story.

Show-jumping is just for horses, right? Wrong, at least not in Sweden. Rabbits have been show-jumping there for over 20 years now, and it's a growing sport. There are over 40 rabbit-jumping clubs in the country, with about 4,000 members, and large crowds attend jumping competitions. The bunnies are held on leashes by their owners and guided around a course of miniature jumping fences. The current champion bunny is named "Flames of Fame". "He knows how great he is," says his owner. "Sometimes he won't start a race until everyone claps."

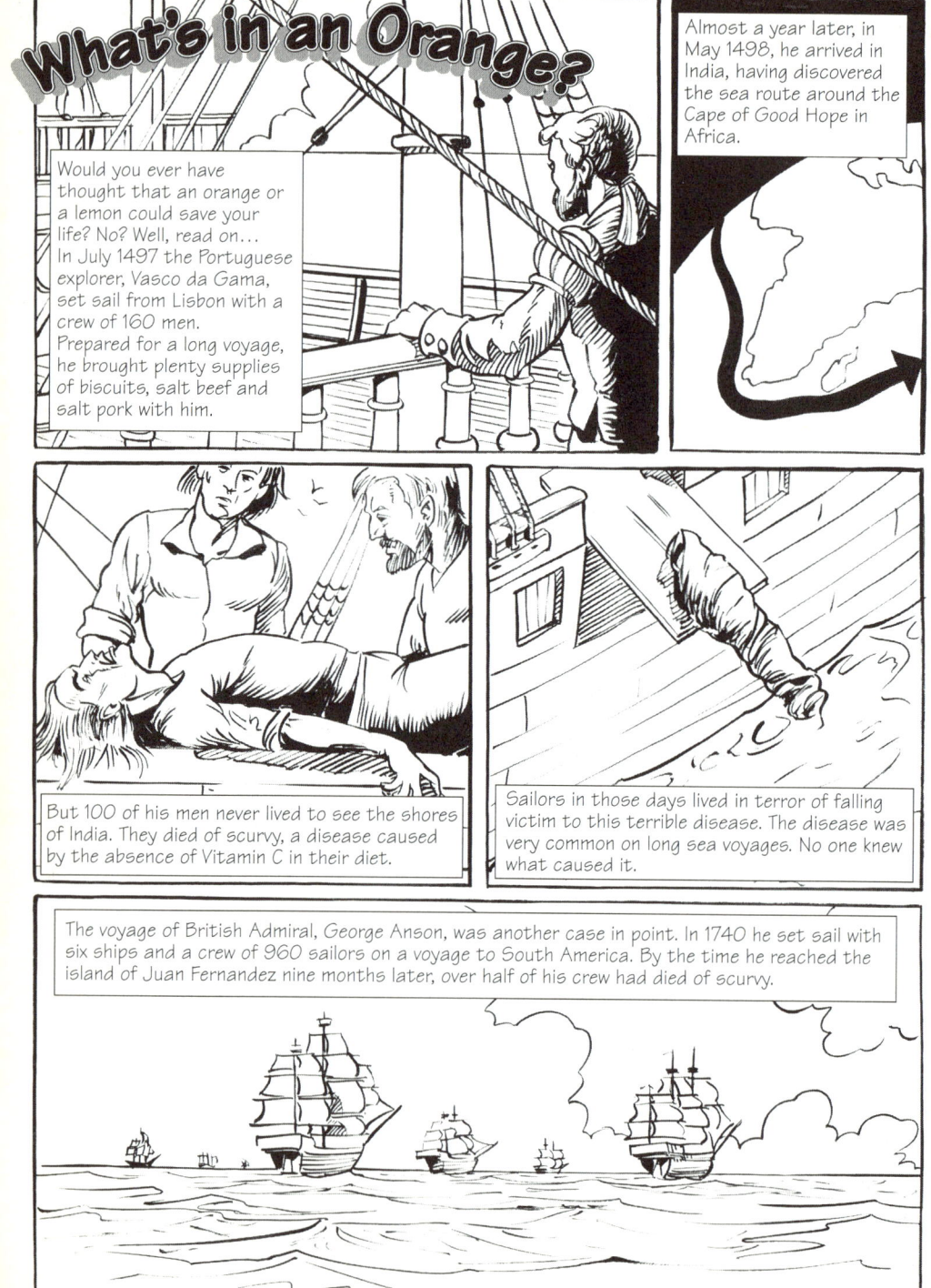

French explorer, Jacques Cartier, might have suffered a similar fate but for the help of some friendly Indians. In 1536, Cartier discovered the St. Lawrence River in Canada.

After the long voyage there, 25 of his men had died of scurvy and many others were seriously ill. An Indian advised them to drink a tea made from the leaves of a certain tree.

The treatment saved the lives of his men. Years later, tests showed that the leaves of the tree contained large amounts of Vitamin C.

It was not until 1747, however, that positive proof of the connection between scurvy and diet was made. James Lind, a doctor in the British Navy, decided to carry out an experiment on twelve patients severely ill with scurvy. All the patients were placed on the same diet, except two, who were given two oranges and one lemon each per day.

After six days, the two who had eaten the fruit had recovered, while the remaining ten were still ill. The vital breakthrough had been made.

Yet it was another forty-eight years before the British Navy ordered that each sailor be given a ration of lime juice every day. After that, the scourge of scurvy came to an end.

BEAT YOUR DRUM

A lot of rock stars play tambourines nowadays. Tambourines make a great sound and are fun to play with. What's more, they're a cinch to make! All you need is: two paper plates; colouring markers (or paint, if you prefer); a stapler, and scissors; some dried beans or nuts or pebbles – anything that will make a good rattle; coloured paper (crêpe).

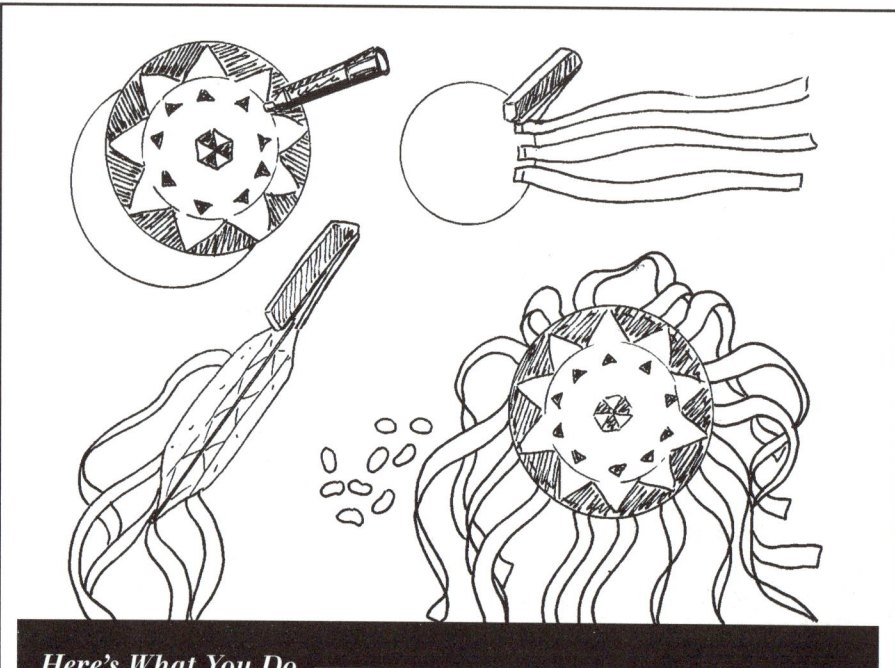

Here's What You Do
1. Use your markers to decorate the plates on the outside.
2. Make streamers by cutting up the coloured crêpe paper into narrow strips. Staple them on to the inside of one of the plates.
3. Staple the two plates together around the rim, but leave a space for putting in the beans.
4. Pour in the beans and then add the final few staples. Your tambourine is made and you're ready to beat it!

ONE-HANDED KNOT

Tie a knot with one hand! Like everything in life, it's easy when you know how. Just follow these four simple steps. All you need is a piece of rope about 60 centimetres long (if you've no rope, a shoelace will do).

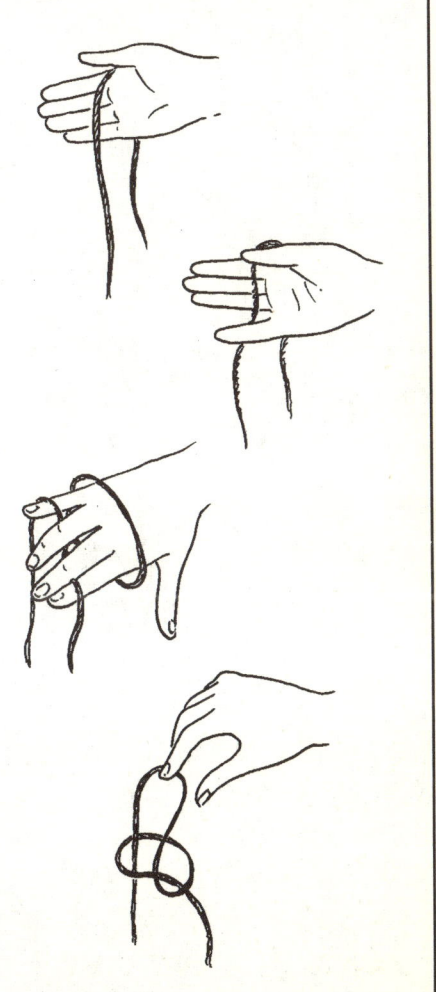

1. Hang the rope over your right hand with the longer part over the palm. [Fig. 1]

2. Clasp the front part of the rope with your little finger and then turn your hand downward. [Fig. 2]

3. Catch hold of the shorter end of the rope with your first and second fingers. [Fig. 3]

4. Give your hand a shake so that the rope falls down in a loop... and the knot is tied. [Fig. 4]

If you practise well, you will be able to perform this trick so quickly that the knot seems to appear as if by magic. Try it!

JOKES JOKES JOKES

What did Fido say when he heard Rex was in the Dog's Home?
Rough.

What should you give a seasick elephant?
Plenty of room.

Waiter, there's a dead fly in my soup.
Yes, it's the heat that kills them.

Why do bees hum?
Because they don't know the words.

Which cake tried to rule the world?
Attila the Bun.

MIXED BAG

ACROSS

1. Game played with a racquet and shuttlecock.
6. The language of ancient Rome.
10. County team known as the cats.
12. Their home ground is Highbury.
14. Richard Branson's airline and record company.
16. Sherlock Holmes' doctor friend.

DOWN

1. Lead singer with U2.
2. Ireland's second TV station.
3. He crossed the Alps with elephants to invade Rome.
4. Napoleon was the emperor of _ _ _ _ _ _
5. Capital of the Philippines.
7. County with Adare and Newcastlewest.
8. Burial places for the pharaohs of ancient Egypt.
9. This company provides Ireland's telephone service.
11. Fish featured in the film *Jaws*.
13. Belfast is on the river _ _ _ _ _.
15. Cardiff, Fishguard and Swansea are in this country.

BRAINSTORM

1. Do sharks have ears?
2. What colour is a sapphire?
3. How many wives did English king Henry the Eighth have?
4. What is a Bombay Duck?
5. Name the capital city of Kenya.
6. What is measured in knots?
7. Who discovered the law of gravity?
8. Finish the saying: "A bird in the hand…"
9. What are people from Finland called?
10. Which precious stone is often used to describe Ireland?

DID YOU KNOW?

When it comes to drinking tea, Ireland holds the world record – 1320 cups per person in one year.

The biggest surviving meteorite in the world is at Hoba West in Namibia, Africa. It weighs 60 tons.

18-year-old Abhishek Jain of India holds the world record for the fastest typist, at 135 words per minute.

BELIEVE IT OR NOT!

Imagine getting into your car, pressing a button, then sitting back and reading the newspaper as your car speeds down the road. Impossible? The experts think otherwise: such a car is only just around the bend, they say. Already millions of dollars are being spent in developing automated highway systems in the US and Japan. The highway of the future will have auto lanes where computer-guided cars will hurtle along at speeds of up to **225km/h**. Chrysler in the US, as well as General Motors, have in fact built a number of robo-cars and are busily testing them on special tracks.

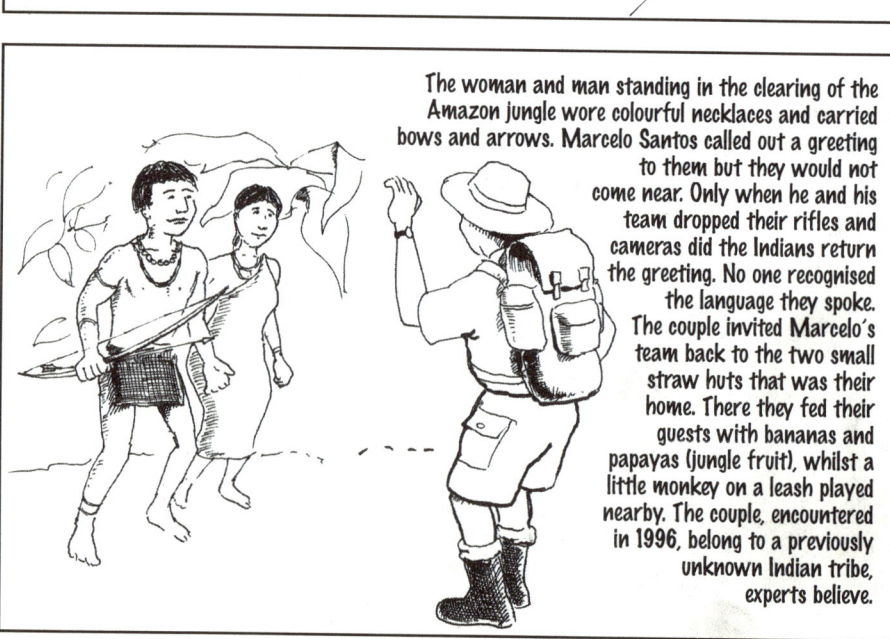

The woman and man standing in the clearing of the Amazon jungle wore colourful necklaces and carried bows and arrows. Marcelo Santos called out a greeting to them but they would not come near. Only when he and his team dropped their rifles and cameras did the Indians return the greeting. No one recognised the language they spoke. The couple invited Marcelo's team back to the two small straw huts that was their home. There they fed their guests with bananas and papayas (jungle fruit), whilst a little monkey on a leash played nearby. The couple, encountered in 1996, belong to a previously unknown Indian tribe, experts believe.

MEET YOUR MATCH

1. Can you make ten by using just nine matches?

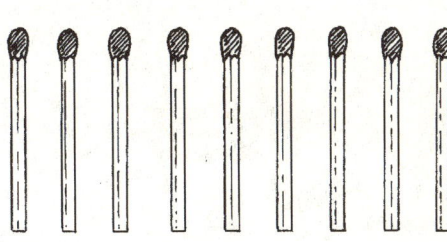

2. Can you make a square by moving just one match?

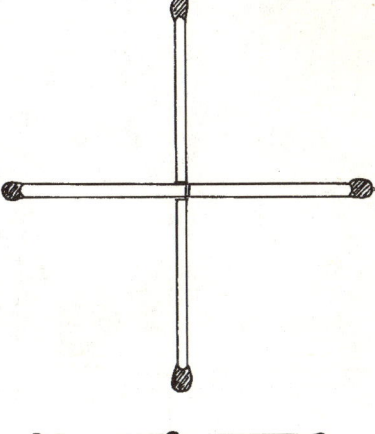

3. By moving two matches can you make seven squares?

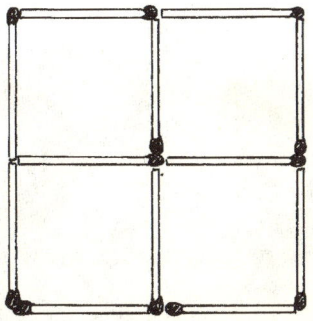

The Bug Man

Have you seen the movie "Jurassic Park"? Remember the 100,000-year-old mosquito fossilised in amber? Well, the person who made that prop is Californian, Steven Kutcher. For over 20 years now he has been supplying Hollywood with every type of creepie-crawlie for every type of movie. When it comes to the movies, Steven is certainly Mr Bug!

Steven has been interested in insects for as long as he can remember. Back in the 1970s he was studying entomology at the University of California when he received a call from the producer of the blockbuster horror movie "Exorcist 2".

Thousands of locusts and grasshoppers were required to co-star with actor Richard Burton. Could he help?

One thing led to another and, before long, Steven was working full time in the movie and TV business.

It was not simply a matter of supplying cockroaches, wasps, bees, ants, flies, spiders to the studio. In one TV movie he was given the almost impossible task of making a wasp fly straight into actor Roddy McDowall's mouth!

How did he do it? First, he removed the wasp's sting...

Then he tied invisible magician's wires to the wasp's body...

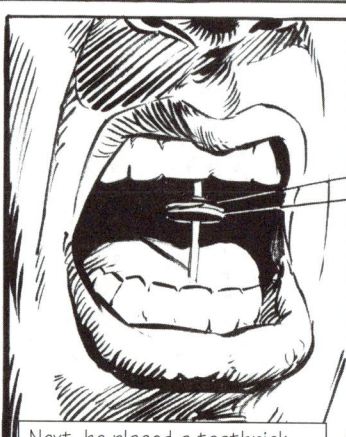

Next, he placed a toothpick pully in the actor's mouth and attached the wires to it...

Then – hey presto! – he pulled the string and the wasp flew right in.

Steven's biggest challenge so far was probably "Arachnophobia", made in 1990. In this horror movie, thousands of spiders attack a small town in the US And as you might expect in a movie of this sort, large numbers of stampeding spiders were required. A tall order, you'll agree...

Steven began by choosing various spiders for trial runs. Instead of running, however, the spiders attacked each other when crowded together!

Luckily, there was one spider with enough sense to do the job properly – the Avendale spider from New Zealand. By using electric fields, wires, and hot and cold floors, Steven was able to make the spiders stampede in any direction he wanted!

Great care has to be taken to ensure that none of these creatures is harmed in any way during filming.

"You can't even harm a maggot nowadays. It's a bit ridiculous, I know, but it makes more work for me."

When he's not working on movies, Stephen gives classes on insects in local schools. Wouldn't you like to be a fly on the wall in that classroom!

THE SOUND OF MUSIC

Try to find the names of 20 musical instruments hidden here.

```
B A G P L I P F S G X V E R T O V O
A R G H A P R L S U Y I H U S L P D
M F S U P I P U B I L O S V S R H Q
C L A R I N E T F L I L B I T P A U
L C E L Q T R E S T P I A O Y L R M
A T W N J R A P R E H N G L E U M B
R E Y L X H A R P K N R P E V R O S
I B A J O N H V I C E V E N I Z N A
M A N D O L I N A L N T I S O R I L
D S E R B N O L N O P R S P L Y C E
L S L H Y T M N O M B U G L E V A R
B O G T E R S T E C A M H B A N T L
R O T R O M B O N E J P A U X A R F
I N F R J U L P D L S E R G Y M U W
N G L P I A M O B L A T M L L J N S
T B U R O U K S T O M V I B O X Z Q
E G A D R U M S G Q I L A J P E R U
O P I N O L S O Q X D L J A H K P W
B R E L J O N A R E P I C C O L O R
E T K R N O P O X C D R O T N S A L
O S A X O P H O N E H F C V E X S A
G U K L E R V A V B A G P I P E S Z
```

TRACK THE TWISTER

A large tornado has just dropped from the sky and the team from the Severe Storms Laboratory are in a hurry to track it down. How fast can you get them there?

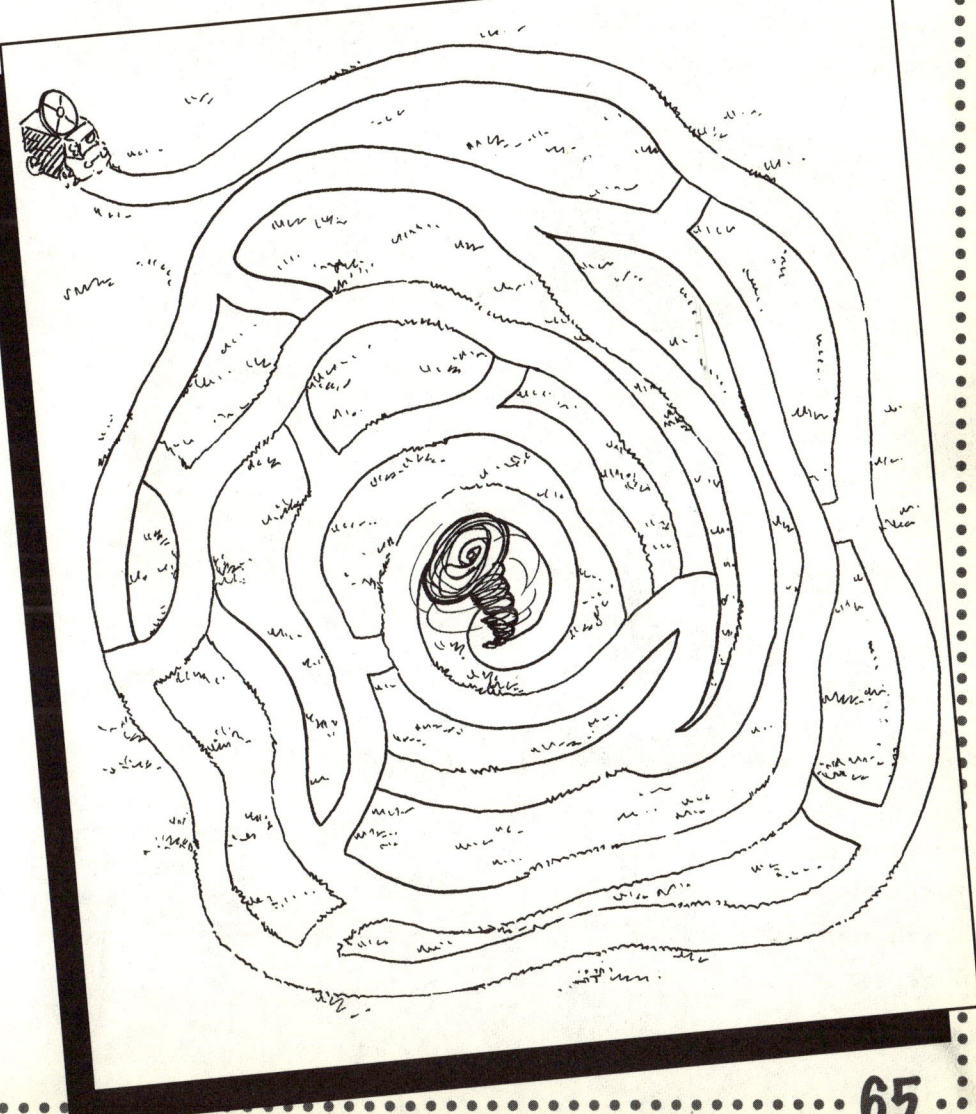

RIDDLES FROM OLD IRELAND

Why is the letter k like a pig's tail?
Because you'll find it at the end of pork.

What date do soldiers dread the most?
April 1st – because it's at the end of a long March.

The man that made it never used it. The man that used it never saw it. What is it?
A coffin.

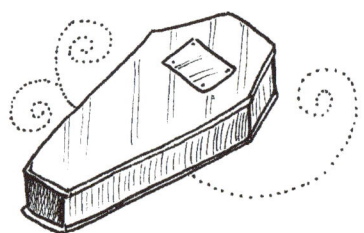

What's as high as a wall, as red as blood, as white as milk and as sweet as honey?
An apple.

What's long and lanky, deaf and dumb, has no legs and yet can run?
A river.

What goes through a rock, a reel, an old cartwheel, a miller's hopper, a sack of pepper, and a cow's shin bone?
Frost.

As round as an apple, as plump as a ball, can climb the church wall and steeple and all. What is it?
The sun.

Why does a donkey prefer thistles to grass?
Because he's an ass.

Patches upon patches, without any stitches, riddle me that and I'll buy you new breeches.
A cabbage patch.

It's black and it's white, and it hops on the road like hailstones. What is it?
A magpie.

What tree is older than all the others?
The elder.

67

BRAINSTORM

1. Which fruit is named after a small New Zealand bird?
2. What is the largest fish in the world?
3. What do the letters ICU (in a hospital) stand for?
4. How many sides has a hexagon?
5. Name Japan's sacred mountain.
6. Who is the only person to score three goals in a World Cup Final?
7. In ancient Rome, who was the Father of the Gods?
8. What did John Holland from County Clare sell to the US Navy in 1900?
9. What is the official address of the British Prime Minister?
10. What is a baby deer called?

DID YOU KNW?

Irish women on average live six years longer than Irish men. The life expectancy for women here is 78 years compared to 72 years for men.

The average height for men in Ireland is 5 feet 8 inches; for women it is 5 feet 3 inches.

American Robert Wadlow (1918 - 1940), was the tallest person in the world. He stood 8 feet 11 inches tall (272 cm).

BELIEVE IT OR NOT!

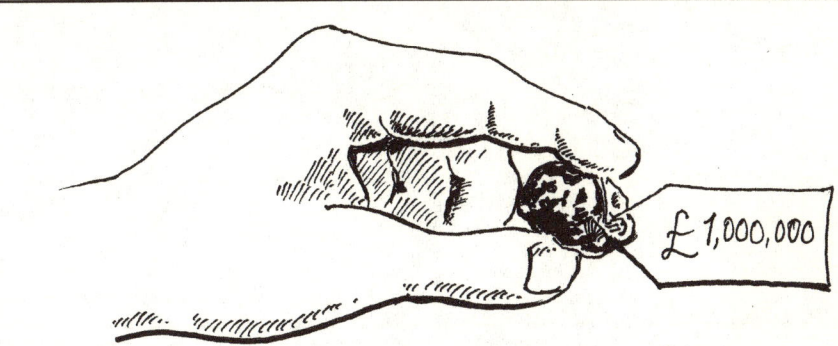

Since the finding of possible traces of life in a meteorite from Mars, the price of meteorites has - like the rock itself - gone sky high. Offers of over £1 million have been made for pieces of Martian meteorite little more than a few grams in size. All you need for meteorite hunting is a walking stick with a magnet taped on to the end. The best places to look for them are: the Nile Delta, the Outback in Australia, the Andes in Chile, and the Arizona Desert. One meteorite hunter from Arizona, Robert Haag, has collected thousands of them, including one multimillion pound rock from Mars.

Garry Kasparov of Russia is the No. 1 chess player in the world. The last time he took on the No. 2 player, he lost only one out of the 19 games. But on the 11th May 1997 something extraordinary happened. Gary sat down to play against an IBM computer, Deeper Blue, and lost! In the sixth and final game, the machine beat the champion in just over an hour, in only nineteen moves. The computer is capable of calculating 400 million chess positions in one second, while Kasparov can work out just four per second. Furthermore, the computer's memory is programmed with all the moves played by chess champions in tournaments over the past 100 years.

It takes Courage!

Unable to walk due to illnes, and unwilling to give up her record attempt, she took lifts. Though she later went back and walked the "missing" kilometres in America, Ffyona still finds it hard to forgive herself...

It takes courage to spend ten years walking 26,400 kilometres around the world. It takes as much courage again to admit at the end of it that you cheated. Ffyona Campbell has now admitted that she cheated during the American leg of her walk.

Whatever way you look at it, though, Ffyona is still the first woman to walk around the world. And that is a rare achievement.

She was just sixteen when she began her epic journey. Her first challenge was to walk the length of Britain, from John O' Groats to Land's End, a distance of 1,600 kilometres. Ffyona – with her hair in dreadlocks – completed it in just 49 days.

Britain is one thing, but imagine walking the length of Africa – a mere 10,000 kilometres! That heroic journey began in Cape Town, South Africa, in April 1991. Each morning, Ffyona rose at dawn, had a mug of tea and some fruit, then hit the road. It wasn't long before she was picking up stones to defend herself against baboons – animals powerful enough to bring down an antelope with their fangs.

Forty-three days later she had crossed the Orange River and was skirting the Kalahari Desert, where big game roamed: springbok, ostrich, and lion...

One night she was woken by the sound of heavy rustling footsteps outside her tent. She crawled out and shone her torch. An enormous bull elephant stood just a few feet away munching on the foliage. Ffyona stayed very quiet and still...

Day after day she walked under the scorching sun. Her feet blistered, her muscles ached, her skin sunburned — not to mention the plague of flies following her everywhere.

By the time she reached Victoria Falls it was time for a rest. Ffyona went micro-lighting over the spectacular Falls...

But how to cross the Sahara? Ffyona wisely chose the western route, hugging the coastline sand-dunes. Her feet sunk in the sand, the hot wind blew relentlessly in her face... though the pink flamingoes were a wonderful sight!

"I made it!"

Finally she entered Morocco and saw the blue Mediterranean. She ran down into the water. She had walked the continent.

MAGIC NUMBERS

Freaky Five
Figure this one out... Think of any number between 1 and 100. Double the number. Add 10 to it. Then divide the number by 2. Finally, subtract the number you thought of in the first place. What are you left with? You said it – FIVE!

Mysterious Nine
Believe it or not, by playing around with a few numbers you can work out what anyone's age is. Here's how:

1. Put a blindfold on. Ask someone, whose age you do not know, to write his or her age on a piece of paper. Let's imagine that you've asked your Aunty Nora to do this – and she's 36 years old.

2. Tell Nora that your lucky number is 90 and that she's to write it below her age, and then add the two numbers.

$$\begin{array}{r} 36 \\ 90 \\ \hline 126 \end{array}$$

3. Now, ask Nora to cross out the digit on the left of her total and to add it instead to the number; thus:

$$\begin{array}{r} 36 \\ 90 \\ \hline \text{[cross out 1] } \cancel{1}26 \\ 1 + 26 = 27 \end{array}$$

4. "What is the total?" you ask Nora.
"27" she replies.

All you have to do now is add the mysterious number 9 to this total... $27+9 = 36$

...and you've figured out how old she is!

KING OF THE JUNGLE

Finish the other half of the lion's face.

JOKES JOKES JOKES

What's orange and sounds like a parrot?
A carrot.

What do you call recently married spiders?
Newly webs.

Mammy, Mammy, I don't want to go to Hawaii.
Stop complaining and keep swimming.

How high is a Chinaman?
As low as his brother.

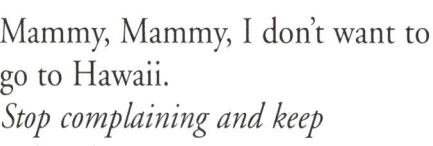

Hey, where are you going with that bag, Lone Ranger?
To the dump, to the dump, to the dump, dump, dump…

"Patrick won't be at school today because he has the flu."

"Could you tell me who's speaking please?"

"This is my father speaking."

"I have my doubts about this plan!"

AMERICANA

ACROSS

4. USA's largest state.
6. FBI = Federal Bureau of _____.
8. They call it the washroom.
12. They call it a fender.
14. JFK's surname.
15. USA's northern neighbour.

DOWN

1. Longest river in the USA.
2. Capital city of the USA.
3. They call it a diaper; we call it a...
5. How many Great Lakes are there?
7. Largest east coast city.
9. Home of the 1996 Olympics.
10. Mountain Range along the west coast.
11. President before Clinton.
13. They put it in their cars and call it gas.

BRAINSTORM

1. Where in the world would you spend drachmas?
2. What is a family of lions called?
3. Who wrote *Charlie and the Chocolate Factory*?
4. What does the Roman numeral M stand for?
5. Name the powerful telescope carried into space by the Space Shuttle *Discovery* in 1990. 
6. By what name was the pirate Edward Teach better known?
7. Who spent 27 years in jail on Robben Island?
8. What does a vulcanologist study?
9. Who was the star of the movie *Home Alone*?
10. What is the meaning of the Japanese word "kamikaze"?

DID YOU KNOW?

The world's smallest fish is the pygmy goby of the Philippines. When fully grown it is only 15 millimetres long – as shown here.

The world's first liquid-fuel rocket was launched by Robert Goddard in 1926. It rose just 12.5 metres off the ground.

Robert Peary, the first person to reach the North Pole, paid a heavy price for his achievement. He lost all his toes due to frostbite.

BELIEVE IT OR NOT!

Are you scared of spiders? The tarantula is one spider which inspires great fear. It can grow to the size of a dinner plate. Not only is it too large to stomp underfoot, but it is also possesses a nasty, venomous bite! One person who loves tarantulas is Rick West in British Columbia, Canada. He is the world's most knowledgeable expert on the spider. He keeps 2,000 of them alive in the basement of his home, as well as a further 3,000 preserved specimens. "They are really very timid creatures," he says. "They rarely bite people."

It was half a metre long, had short front limbs, long hind limbs, long tail and – most remarkable of all – was partly covered with feathers. Li Yumin, the Chinese farmer who dug it up in 1996, thought he had discovered a dragon. But Philip Currie, the first western scientist to examine the 120-million-year-old fossil, had a different view. "It's a little feathered dinosaur," he announced. Some dinosaurs, it seems, were warm bloooded and needed feathers to keep themselves warm. Sinosauropteryx is the latest and most startling evidence pointing to a definite link between dinosaurs and birds.

BRAINTEASERS

BRAINTEASERS

1. As I was going to St Ives
   I met a man with seven wives
   Each wife had seven cats
   Each cat has seven kits.
   How many were going to St Ives?

2. Give the name of a sport which is popular all over the world and begins with a T (It's not Tennis).

3. What word is made shorter by lengthening it?

4. Can you pick the odd one out of the following: red, orange, pink, yellow, green, blue, indigo, violet.

5. Pointing to a photo of a man, Joan turns to her father and says, "That man's mother is my mother's mother-in-law." Who is in the photograph?

6. What will be the date of the first day of the next century?

7. What was the name of the American president in 1953?

TONGUE-TWISTERS

How fast can you say the following?

"Peter Piper picked a peck of pickled pepper."

"Around the rugged rocks the ragged rascal ran."

"The sixth sheik's sixth sheep is sick."

"She sells seashells on the seashore."

Storm Clouds Over Everest

Since Edmund Hillary and Tenzing Norgay conquered Everest in 1953, many other mountaineers have climbed the 8,848 metres to the summit of the world's tallest mountain. On one famous day in 1993, 40 people reached the top. When the weather is fine, there can be so many climbers that the teams have to queue up to climb the final leg.

Many climbers bring their mobile phones with them so they can call up their families and friends from the tip-top of the world.

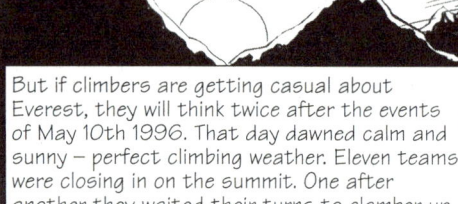

But if climbers are getting casual about Everest, they will think twice after the events of May 10th 1996. That day dawned calm and sunny – perfect climbing weather. Eleven teams were closing in on the summit. One after another they waited their turns to clamber up on to the roof of the world. By mid-day, twenty people had made it to the top.

But when US surgeon, Seaborn Weathers, turned to gaze across the majestic Himalayas stretched out below him, something bothered him. There, on the horizon, storm clouds were gathering.

Weathers was a dedicated mountaineer, but an amateur one. His one great ambition had been to climb Everest. Now as the storm clouds swept in, his dream turned into a nightmare. The winds howled and the snow whipped mercilessly. The temperature dropped to a deadly -95° C. It was time to descend – and fast!

Seaborn Weathers' clothing was designed to protect him only to -60° C. Unable to move, he lay down in the snow. It seemed he had no chance. The other climbers left him behind. When the first survivors fought their way down to base camp, a message was relayed to Mrs Weathers in Texas that her husband was lost.

But Weathers refused to die. Somehow he managed to get up on his feet again. Helped by a lull in the storm, he started to stagger down the mountain. On his way, he met up with another climber Makalu Gau, from Taiwan. He, too, had been left behind for dead.

Meanwhile, a Nepalese helicopter pilot Lieut. Colonel Madan was scouring the Everest slopes for survivors. His eye caught something high on the mountain above. It was a large cross the desperate climbers had drawn on the ice with red lemonade. At 6,000 metres they were almost beyond the reach of a helicopter. At that altitude the air is so thin that it can barely give enough lift to the chopper's rotary blades.

Yet the daring Lieut. Colonel flew to the rescue. First he picked up Gau and flew him to base camp.

Then he returned and saved Seaborn Weathers. It was the second-highest helicopter rescue of all time.

BANANAS!

You might be driven bananas trying to find the 20 fruits and 20 vegetables hidden in this wordsearch. They read across, down, up and diagonally. This is the hardest wordsearch in the book, so go on, have a go!

```
B O D O T E K I L U O Y T A H W
L L J A S U V K L H S I V A R G
E B A N T U R S Q P O J N S I N
T V B C D E S N I Q T L R W O L
T S Q Z K O K N I Z A E D M P O
U P L U M B A W A P P L E A I D
C J E I D C E W D P J L H N N Q
E G Y A H J T R E J R K A G S U
R P D A C E K P R N F I E O R D
I J D S V H Q F O Y B P C E A N
N E A I C H O L P L A H D O P U
L G W B A K E S P R E O S W T O
P I D W R M Q U G R T E V K N F
K F M Y R P E A R A C U K I E T
I A J E O H V Y T A R A O M P O
N F T U T K U O B E L N L O E N
G A E Y S T P B R E E V E O L S
W C L A N E A E A U E S N R P I
H O P M G G T A X R K P T H P R
A R P N E R S N T Y B P I S A A
T N A R Q B A N A N A V L U E D
Y R B R O C C O L I M D A M N I
O C E L E R Y G E D A J S E I S
U H A V E T A V O C A D O G P H
```

COIN MAGIC ∗∗∗

Here's a really neat trick that will amaze your friends. You place a 20p coin (showing the harp) in the palm of your right hand, then slap the coin down on to the palm of your left hand... and yet the coin still turns up harps!

How's it done?

1. Place the coin in your palm, in the position shown. Tell your friends to look closely at the harp.

2. Now, as you close and raise your hand, you can use your thumb as a lever to flick the coin over without anyone seeing it. It's worth practising this a few times to get it right. Speed is the key to success in magic.

3. Then slap the coin down on to your other palm and hey presto!... the harp shows again!

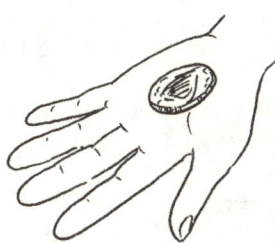

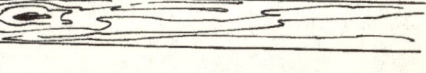

JOKES JOKES JOKES

What is the biggest mouse in the world?
Hippopotamouse.

Which Italian mouse became a dictator?
Mousellini.

Which mouse was a famous musical composer?
Mousezart.

Which famous mouse once starred as a reindeer in a Disney cartoon?
Mickey Moose.

What did the mice do on the First Aid Course?
They practised mouse to mouse resuscitation.

Where do Russian mice prefer to live?
Mousecow.

What would you call the best known mouse in the world?
Famouse.

Which fish was a wild west outlaw?
Billy the Cod.

What would you call a crazy duck?
Quackers.

What did the art thief say when arrested?
I've been framed.

Doctor, I know you're thinking I've put on too much weight. Why do you say that?
Because when you were checking my tonsils, you said, "Open your mouth and say moo…"

Dog 1: What's your name?
Dog 2: Fido. What's yours?
Dog 1: I'm not sure. I think it's Down Boy.

BRAINSTORM

1. How many wings has a bee?
2. What type of wood is used for making the black keys on a piano?
3. Who won the 1997 World Snooker Final?
4. Finish this saying, "One swallow…"
5. What was so special about the *Viking 1* spacecraft?
6. All snowflakes are symmetrical. How many sides do they have?
7. How big is an Olympic-size pool and how many lanes does it have?
8. Which South American vulture has a wing span of three metres?
9. Give the more common name for ascorbic acid.
10. What did Christopher Cockerell invent?

DID YOU KNOW?

The 825-year-old Leaning Tower at Pisa in Italy leans 5.5 degrees from perpendicular.

The human body contains 4.5 litres of blood.

Scientists have discovered that dolphins call each other by name.

HEY JOE!

YO BILL

BELIEVE IT OR NOT!

Imagine trying to cross the whole of Australia from north to south. That's what John Stuart, a Scotsman, set out to do in 1862. The Australian government had offered a prize of £10,000 as a reward and Stuart was determined to pick it up.
Two years earlier, Robert Burke and Charles Wills had made the attempt. They had got within sight of the sea but had been forced to turn back. On the way back, they died of exhaustion. Stuart chose a different route and succeeded. He was so exhausted he had to be carried back in a sling tied between two horses.

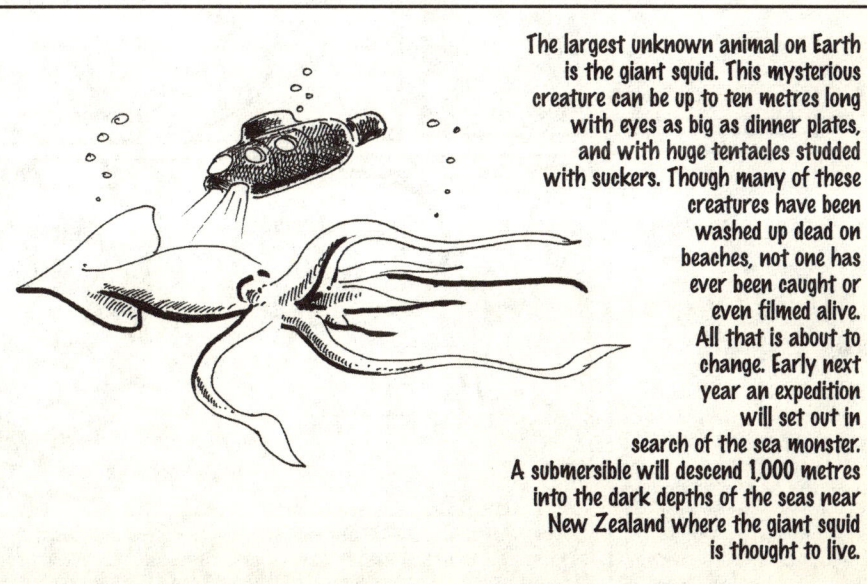

The largest unknown animal on Earth is the giant squid. This mysterious creature can be up to ten metres long with eyes as big as dinner plates, and with huge tentacles studded with suckers. Though many of these creatures have been washed up dead on beaches, not one has ever been caught or even filmed alive. All that is about to change. Early next year an expedition will set out in search of the sea monster. A submersible will descend 1,000 metres into the dark depths of the seas near New Zealand where the giant squid is thought to live.

If it Glitters, it's Gold

Mel Fisher was a treasure hunter who dreamed of finding the long lost Atocha. In the 1960s he spent four luckless years searching for it.

In September 1622 a fleet of 28 galleons set sail from Cuba for Spain. All the ships were carrying treasure. The richest of them all was the Atocha. They were off the coast of Florida when a hurricane struck. Eight of the ships went down, the Atocha among them.

Not one for giving up easily, he hired a historian, Eugene Lyons, and told him to look for clues in 17th-century Spanish maritime records. Lyons did just that and found a report from a Spanish captain who had salvaged one of the wrecks in 1622. It gave the location of the disaster.

"This is it!"

"You have been looking in the wrong place. The Atocha sank 100 miles to the south of your search zone."

So Mel Fisher went back to work. Day after day, from dawn to dusk, he criss-crossed the sea in his boat, dragging a magnetometer through the water. The magnetometer was powerful enough to detect any iron lying on the sea floor.

"Ok Don. Down you go if you're all geared up and checked out."

"On my way, boss."

On a day in June 1971 the magnetometer suddenly started buzzing. Something was down there. Fisher sent a diver to investigate – but nothing was found. So he decided to switch on the propellors, to wash away some of the sand below. Then, he sent down another diver, Don Kinkaid.

The propellors had cleared away a hole in the sand. There, Kinkaid found a large iron anchor. Then something else caught his eye.

I thought it was brass at first, then suddenly I knew it was gold. I fought against the falling sand and dug frantically with my hands and ended up with an eight-foot gold chain.

That's it, boss. There's only sand left down there now. We've cleaned the place out.

The first treasure from the Atocha had been found. Over the following days many more gold chains, gold bars and coins were found. But soon everything dried up, and no more finds were made.

Still Fisher went on searching, for years and years...

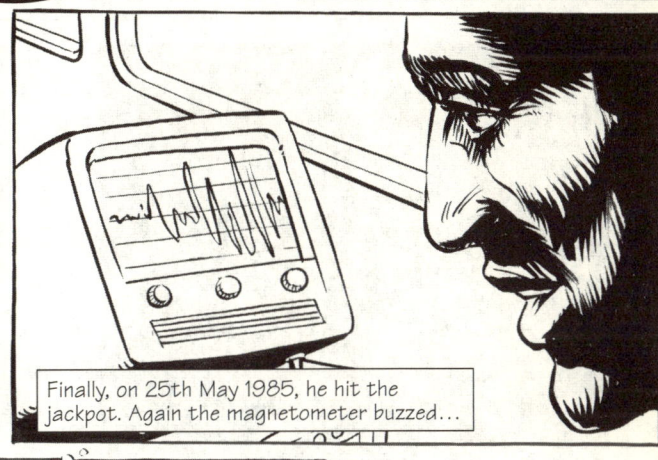

Finally, on 25th May 1985, he hit the jackpot. Again the magnetometer buzzed...

YES!

Again the propellor was switched on, and a diver, Susan Nelson, went down. She swam back up with four large gold bars. This time they had found the whole treasure-load of the Atocha.

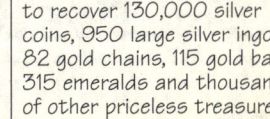

Fisher and his divers went on to recover 130,000 silver coins, 950 large silver ingots, 82 gold chains, 115 gold bars, 315 emeralds and thousands of other priceless treasures.

CLOWNING AROUND

Bored? Why don't you and your friends paint each other's faces as clowns? The painting is great fun and the clowning around is even better! All you need are:

1. Some water-based face paints. (It's important that the paints are water-based, so they can be easily washed off afterwards.)
2. One wide paintbrush, and one fine paintbrush.

1st Step
Paint a big red mouth.
Then paint a red cirle on the nose as shown.

2nd Step
Ask your friend to keep his or her eyes closed.
Paint blue oval shapes over his or her eyebrows and eyelids.

3rd Step
Paint a white outline around the mouth and the eyes.

4th Step
Use the fine paintbrush to add the lines around the eyes as shown.
Put some gel in his or her hair now to get it to stick out... borrow some over-sized old clothes... and it's circus time!

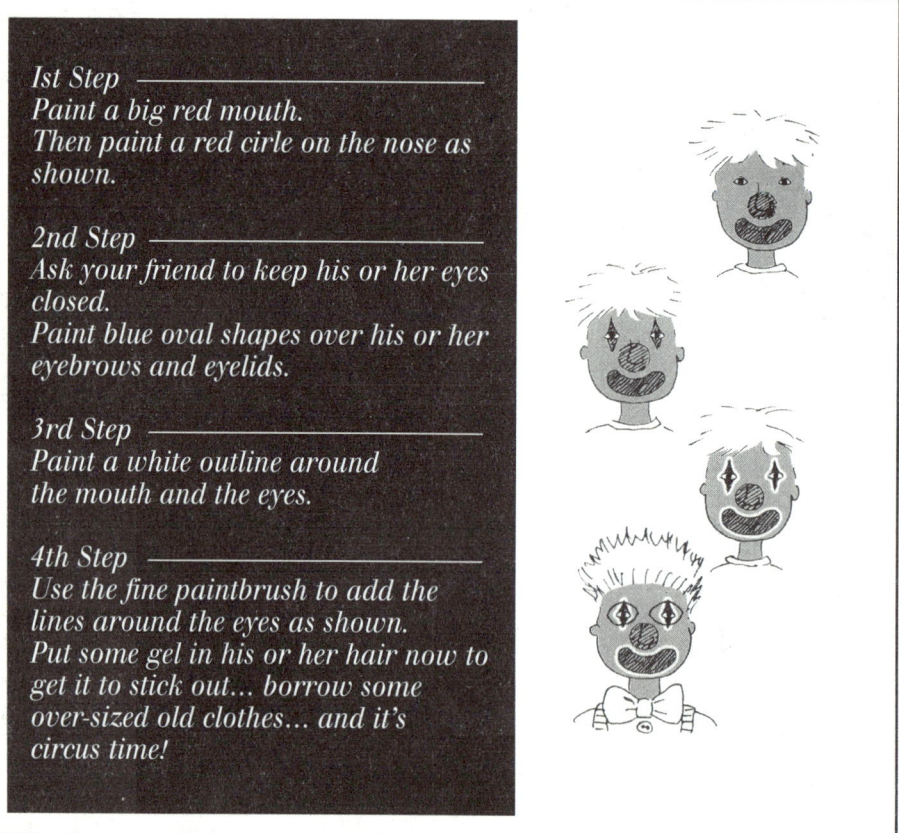

WHAT'S THE DIFFERENCE?

Spot 12 differences between these two pictures.

JOKES JOKES JOKES

What's the difference between a baby monkey and a matterbaby?
What's a matterbaby?
Nothing, what's wrong with you?

How do you make a Mexican chilli?
Send him to the North Pole.

How many ears has Captain Kirk of Star Trek got?
Three: the left ear, the right ear, and the final frontier.

Knock, knock
Who's there?
Adolph.
Adolph who?
Adolph ball hit me on the head.

Knock, knock
Who's there?
Dishwasher.
Dishwasher who?
Disherwasher way I shpoke when I losht my falsh teeth.

"I thought Gino said this plan was idiot-proof."

"Well, no sign of an Anaconda. We may as well pack it in for today."

HOSPITAL HEALTH

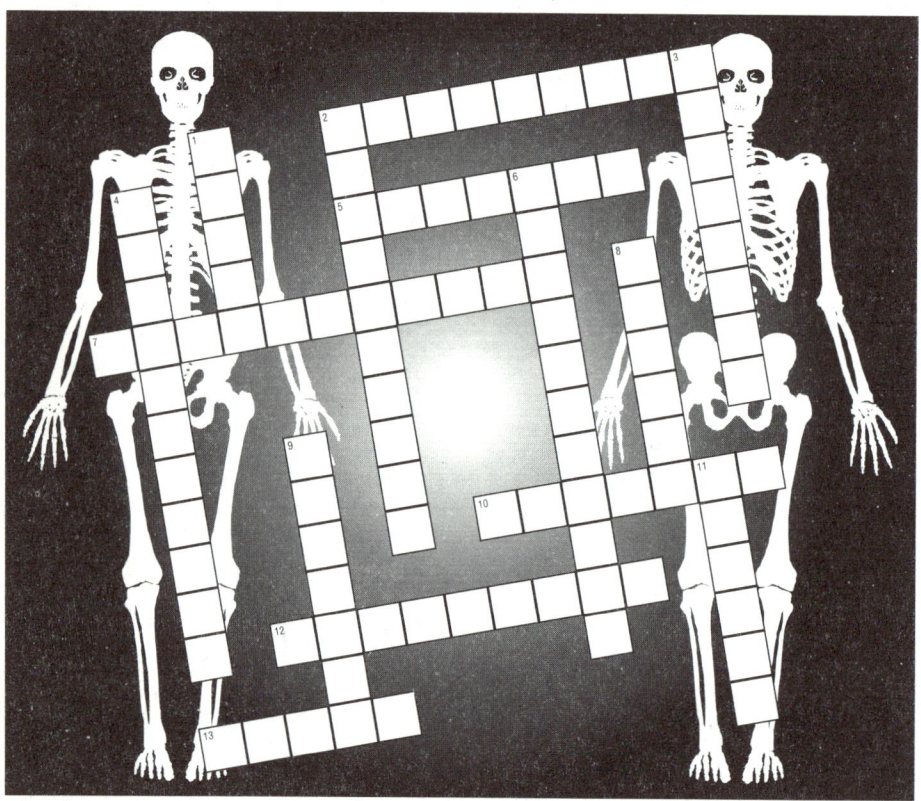

ACROSS

2. Vehicle to bring you to hospital in a hurry.
5. Where operations are performed.
7. Used to listen to heartbeat.
10. What surgeons do.
12. Word that says patient has improved.
13. Nurses hold your wrist to time this.

DOWN

1. It pumps blood around our bodies.
2. Something which kills germs.
3. The activity we need to stay healthy.
4. Where the Red Cross was founded.
6. It measures temperature.
8. The liquid we have in our mouths to help us digest our food.
9. What you have when you're not well. An _ _ _ _ _ _ _.
11. It attaches muscle to the bone.

BRAINSTORM

1. Does the Earth spin from east to west or from west to east?
2. Which famous athlete stars in the movie *Space Jam*?
3. Which waterfalls are on the Zambezi River?
4. Which is the only bird that is able to fly backwards?
5. She died in Rouen, France in 1431 and was made a saint in 1920. Who was she?
6. In which street in New York is the US Stock Exchange located?
7. What is a beaver's home called?
8. What does a speleologist study?
9. What name is given to a 25th wedding anniversary?
10. What colour is a ruby?

DID YOU KNOW?

Irish pop star of the Fifties, Ruby Murray, had five top twenty hits in the charts at the one time. This has only been equalled by The Beatles.

Denim clothing takes its name from a town in France, de Nimes.

In October 1922 Miss G.W. Ballantine caught a salmon on the River Tay in Scotland. It weighed 28 kilograms, setting a UK record that still stands.

BELIEVE IT OR NOT!

In 1887 a Swedish schoolboy was looking through a pile of his grandmother's letters when he spotted something unusual. A "three skilling" stamp on one of the letters was yellow in colour, not green as it ought to have been. The young stamp collector sold it for very little money, and over the years the stamp passed from one owner to another. The little piece of paper, nicknamed the "Swedish error", is now the most valuable postage stamp in the world. Last year at an auction in Switzerland, a Swedish businessman paid £1.4 million for it. The auctioneer was David Feldman from Dublin.

It's 150 years since gold was discovered in Australia, but there are people who still go out in search of it.

Mark Creasy had been prospecting for gold in Australia for 25 years with little or no success.
Still, he never gave up. Driving a beaten-up 1968 landrover and living on a diet of rice and tinned fish, he spent 70 hours each week at his job. His perseverance finally paid off when he struck gold in the Yandal Belt, Western Australia. In 1994 he sold his share for £80 million, making him the country's most successful gold prospector ever.

PUZZLE IT OUT

Try to draw this shape without lifting your pen off the page or without going over any line twice.

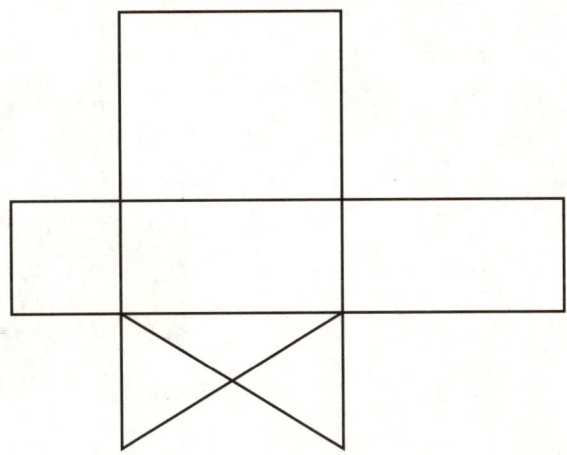

TOTAL BRAINTEASER

Can you rearrange the numbers so that any line of numbers added together will give the same total?

"It's like, totally amazing... just brilliant... awesome!"

"I've seen it three times already!"

But this was a movie that every girl and boy wanted to see – about a dozen times.

"Star Wars" became an overnight success, not just in America but all around the world.

Two sequels quickly followed, "The Empire Strikes Back", and "Return of the Jedi". Between them, the three movies have already earned a stunning $1.3 billion.

This year sees the 20th anniversary of "Star Wars". To celebrate it, it had been planned to show the movie in just a few cinemas around the US. But when Hollywood came up with $15 million to spend on reworking all three movies, George Lucas could not resist.

"Excellent!"

Outdated special effect scenes were spruced up. New computer-generated creatures were added to the backgrounds. Extra spaceships were added to the battle scenes.

With a great fanfare, the three movies were rereleased.

"Star Wars" has now outstripped "E.T." as the highest-earning movie ever. And George Lucas is still dreaming – three new "Star Wars" movies are already in the pipeline...

JOKES JOKES JOKES

What's worse than finding a worm in your apple?
Finding half a worm in your apple.

What do you get when you cross an elephant with a kangaroo?
A lot of damage in Australia.

What's the difference between a shop and an elephant's bottom?
I don't know.
Well, I'm not sending you on a message to the shops!

Doctor, Doctor, I keep thinking I'm a pair of curtains.
You've got to stop this nonsense and pull yourself together.

Aunty, Aunty, when are you going to do your trick?
What trick is that, dear?
Daddy says you can drink like a fish.

Girl: Teacher gave out to me today because I didn't know where the Pyramids were.
Dad: Well, you should try and remember where you put things.

Boy: Teacher said I should get an encyclopaedia.
Mum: No. I think you should walk to school like everyone else.

Teacher: Order, order, children!
Mary: I'll have an ice-pop please, Sir.

Teacher: John, what did David do to Goliath?
John: I don't want to snitch on anyone, Miss.

Teacher: Anne, what happened when the wheel was invented?
Anne: There was a revolution, Sir.

Teacher: Paul, name three members of the cat family.
Paul: Daddy cat, Mammy cat, and Baby cat.

THE RIGHT ORDER

The six words below have been put in the right order in the grid to give two new words (CHANCE, ORDERS) which can be read in the vertical columns 1 and 2.

    CARRY   NIECE   CHOIR,
    EASED   HERON ADDER

	1	2		
C	H	O	I	R
H	E	R	O	N
A	D	D	E	R
N	I	E	C	E
C	A	R	R	Y
E	A	S	E	D

Now do the same with each of the following:

NANNY   ROPES   CHESS
PROUD   ELDER   IDEAL

EASED   FORCE   INNER
CAKES   FAINT   ORDER

KICKS   EARLY   EASED
TRADE   TEMPT   LUPIN

DERBY   UNION   MISTY
EVENT   BATHE   NAMED

LAIRS   EVENT   RANGE
WATER   FABLE   OUTER

SINCE   VIDEO   LEARN
ONION   GAMES   EXERT

102

Trick Your Friends

Try this trick on your friends —
This trick works nine times out of ten. Go up to your friend and tell her that you are going to make her say the word "yellow". She'll of course answer: "Let's see you try."
Begin by asking her four or five easy questions like "What day is it? What is the capital of Russia?" and so on.
You then quickly ask: "What are the colours on the Irish flag?"
Your friend replies: "Green, white and orange."
You say (pretending really hard that you have caught her out): "There you are – I said I'd make you say 'orange'!"
Your friend: "No you didn't. You said 'yellow'."
You: "You've just said it!"

Here's another tricky one —
Before you try it on your friends, try it on yourself...
Carefully read the first two sentences below and then see if you can complete the third one:
1. Wind in the the Willows.
2. Once in a a blue moon.
3. Flash in the ....
Now check the answer!

MAKE YOUR OWN ICE CREAM

Here's a simple recipe for making your own ice cream. All you need is:
  One 400g can of evaporated milk
  About 400g of fresh fruit, such as raspberries, or strawberries – choose any soft summer fruit you like!
  100g icing sugar
  A sieve, a mixing bowl, and a whisk.

1. Leave the can of milk in the fridge overnight so that it's nice and cold. Then empty the milk into a bowl and whisk it until it's thick and frothy.
2. Add the icing sugar to the milk, whisking it in well.
3. Use a spoon to press the fruit – raspberries – through the sieve. This makes what's called a raspberry purée.
4. Now, add the raspberry purée to the bowl, stirring it in well.
5. The mixture is now ready for the ice-making compartment of your fridge or freezer. While the mixture freezes over the next few hours, stir it a couple of times.

Now, for the nice part!
Sprinkle your ice cream with some flake chocolate and serve...

SOLUTIONS

Brainstorm (page 5)
1. The Royal python holds the record at 10.7m (35 feet) in length **2.** The escudo is the currency of Portugal **3.** elver **4.** Lazlo Biro from Hungary **5.** Stockholm, Sweden. **6.** Elvis Presley. Graceland was the name of the mansion where he lived in Memphis, Tennessee. **7.** In Venice, Italy. The gondola is a long narrow boat used on the canals there. **8.** The President of the United States. **9.** The prophet Mohammed **10.** Deeper Blue (to find out more about this amazing chess battle, turn to page 69)

Funny Money (page 7)
1. Five Makes Seven: Pick up coins 1 and 5 and place them on top of coin 3 (the middle coin). There is now an equal number of coins in both lines.

Another solution is to move coin 5 beside coin 7 and move coin 1 to where coin 5 was.

2. Harps and Fish: slide the two coins out from the bottom row, bringing them to the position shown above the top row... and in one movement, push them down (in the direction of the arrow) so that all the coins are rearranged to make a square again. Problem solved.

The Big Screen (page 11)
Batman, Jaws, Star Wars, Space Jam, Matilda, Robin Hood, Aladdin, Independence Day, Top Gun, Under Siege, Michael Collins, Ransom, Jerry Maguire, Braveheart, Daylight, Twins, Ghost, Waterworld, Superman, Pinocchio.

105

Brainstorm (page 14)
1. Batman 2. Champagne 3. In San Francisco, California, USA 4. Leonardo da Vinci 5. Caesar Augustus, Emperor of Rome (a nephew of Julius Caesar) 6. An eagle 7. Poisons 8. Adi Dassler was an athlete who made a pair of runners in 1920 and founded the Adidas company. 9. Ten sides 10. Alice in Wonderland (from *Alice in Wonderland*)

A Riddle from Ancient Times (page 19)
After standing there a long time pondering, the merchant realised the solution to his problem. He picked up the golden balls and began practising a trick he had learned as a young man. After a few hours' practice, he was ready to step on to the bridge. And as he did so, he began juggling the three golden balls… and so made his way safely across the bridge.

How Many? (page 22)
Across: 2. Ten 4. Fifteen 7. Nine 9. Eleven 10. Thirty 13. One 14. Fourteen
Down: 1. Twelve 2. Twenty 3. Three 5. Thirteen 6. Hundred 8. Five 11. Two 12. Four

Brainstorm (page 23)
1. There are 50 stars, one for each of the States. 2. The Philippines 3. Adder 4. By feeling the small diamond-shaped ridge on the end of the note 5. A comet is made of ice. 6. Tarmacadam 7. Both of them starred as James Bond in the movies. 8. One hundred 9. Twister 10. Michael Carruth in Boxing

Fashion Crazy (page 25)
cap, gloves, jeans, jacket, trousers, dress, teeshirt, blouse, socks, tie, cardigan, shoes, sandals, boots, sweatshirt, runners, coat, tracksuit, shorts, jersey. LEVIS, BENETTON, NIKE, REEBOK, ADIDAS.

Famous Pairs (page 29)
Fred Flintstone and Barney Rubble… Tom and Jerry… Batman and Robin… Cain and Abel… Lois Lane and Clark Kent (Superman)… Adam and Eve… Zig and Zag… Jack and Jill… Romulus and Remus (founders of Rome)… Marks and Spencer… Samson and Delilah (Samson was the strong man in the Bible who

knocked down the walls of the temple; Delilah was his wife)… Beavis and Butt-head… Anthony and Cleopatra (Cleopatra was the Egyptian queen who fell in love with the Roman general, Anthony. They were defeated in battle by Augustus in 30 BC)… Hansel and Gretel… Laurel and Hardy… David and Goliath… Tweedledum and Tweedledee… Jeckyll and Hyde.

Neil Armstrong and Edwin Buzz Aldrin (the first pair to walk on the Moon, 21st July 1969)… Edmund Hillary and Tenzing Norgay (they were first to climb Mount Everest, in 1953)… Alan Hale and Thomas Bopp (they spotted the Hale-Bopp comet first, in July 1995)… Gottlieb Daimler and Karl Benz (the two Germans who invented the motor engine, independently)… John Alcock and Arthur Brown (the first to fly non-stop across the Atlantic, in 1919. They flew from Newfoundland to Ireland)… David Livingstone and Henry Stanley (Stanley travelled through the Congo in Africa in search of Livingstone who had been feared lost. He finally found him in 1871. "Doctor Livingstone, I presume," Stanley famously said on meeting the long-lost explorer.)

Brainstorm (page 32)
1. "That's one small step for man, one giant leap for mankind." **2.** There are six strings on a guitar. **3.** Albania **4.** Cranium **5.** The Aztecs lived in Mexico **6.** The gift of the "blarney" – the gift of eloquence (fluent speech) **7.** A supernova is a star that suddenly explodes. **8.** The Titanic in 1912 **9.** Snooker **10.** The poet WB Yeats

Landmarks (page 40)
Across: 6. Taj Mahal **8.** Eiffel **10.** Empire State **13.** Everest **14.** Big Ben
Down: 1. Los Angeles **2.** Colosseum **3.** Great Wall **4.** Leaning **5.** Buckingham **7.** New York **9.** Egypt **11.** Berlin **12.** Athens

Brainstorm (page 41)
1. Stamp Addressed Envelope **2.** Japan **3.** Throat **4.** Five players per team **5.** The Star Spangled Banner **6.** A dromedary camel has just one hump, while a bactrian camel has two. **7.** Mercedes **8.** The 14th of February **9.** Cleopatra (after her army was defeated by the Romans under Augustus in 30 BC, she took her own life by means of a snake bite). **10.** A poisonous jellyfish

Sportsearch (page 46)
hockey, badminton, archery, cycling, judo, fencing, gymnastics, boxing, squash, bowling, soccer, karate, swimming, rugby, skiing, surfing, tennis, golf, orienteering, hurling

Pop Puzzle (page 47)
BLUR, BOYZONE, SPICE GIRLS, OASIS, THE FUGEES, BON JOVI, KULA SHAKER.
MADONNA, BONO, ELVIS, PRINCE, MICHAEL JACKSON, CELINE DION, JAMIROQUAI.

Brainstorm (page 50)
1. Tiger Woods **2.** The elephant **3.** Spiders **4.** The Vatican City – only 738 people live there. **5.** Mercury **6.** Norway has a border with Russia. **7.** The light bulb **8.** Deer **9.** Steven Spielberg **10.** The Koran is the holy book of the Moslems.

Mixed Bag (page 58)
Across: 1. Badminton **6.** Latin **10.** Kilkenny **12.** Arsenal **14.** Virgin **16.** Watson
Down: 1. Bono **2.** Network Two **3.** Hannibal **4.** France **5.** Manila **7.** Limerick **8.** Pyramids **9.** Telecom **11.** Shark **13.** Lagan **15.** Wales

Brainstorm (page 59)
1. Yes, all sharks have a pair of inner ears, connected to the outside world by tiny tubes. **2.** This precious stone is blue in colour. **3.** Six wives **4.** A fish **5.** Nairobi **6.** The speed of a boat or ship **7.** Sir Isaac Newton in 1687 **8.** "...is worth two in the bush." **9.** Finns **10.** Emerald

Meet Your Match (page 61)

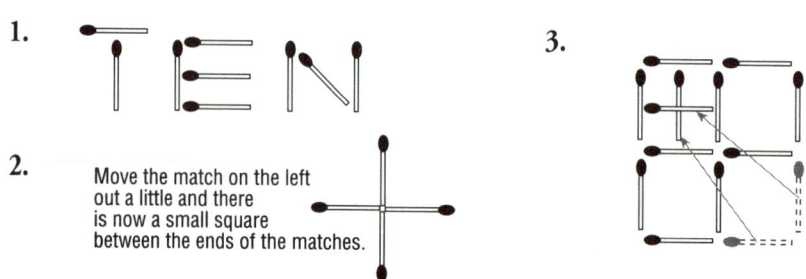

2. Move the match on the left out a little and there is now a small square between the ends of the matches.

The Sound of Music (page 64)
guitar, violin, harp, clarinet, flute, trumpet, trombone, drums, cello, saxophone, bugle, harmonica, mandolin, banjo, bagpipes, bassoon, piano, xylophone, piccolo, oboe

Brainstorm (page 68)
1. Kiwi **2.** The Whale Shark – it can be up to 15 metres long and weighs 18,000 kilograms. **3.** Intensive Care Unit **4.** Six sides **5.** Mount Fuji **6.** Geoff Hurst for England against West Germany in 1966 **7.** Jupiter **8.** He sold the submarine he had designed. It was the US Navy's first submarine, and it was named the *Holland* after its inventor. **9.** Number 10, Downing Street, London. **10.** A fawn

Americana (page 76)
Across: 4. Alaska **6.** Investigation **8.** Bathroom **12.** Bumper **14.** Kennedy **15.** Canada
Down: 1. Mississippi **2.** Washington **3.** Nappy **5.** Five **7.** New York **9.** Atlanta **10.** Rocky **11.** Bush **13.** Petrol

Brainstorm (page 77)
1. Greece **2.** A pride **3.** Roald Dahl **4.** 1,000 **5.** The Hubble telescope **6.** Blackbeard **7.** Nelson Mandela **8.** Volcanoes (Vulcan was the ancient Roman god of fire.) **9.** Macaulay Culkin **10.** Kamikaze means "Divine Wind". (It refers to the hurricane which wrecked the fleet of the Mongols attempting to invade Japan in 1281.)

Brainteasers (page 79)
1. The answer is one. Only one person, the "I", was going to St Ives – all the rest were coming from St Ives. **2.** Golf – it begins with a Tee **3.** Short **4.** The odd one out is pink – all the others are colours of the rainbow. **5.** Her father **6.** January 1st, 2001 **7.** Bill Clinton – he went by that name back in 1953 too!

Bananas! (page 82)
blackberry, watermelon, plum, orange, peach, lime, pear, kiwi, avocado, apricot, date, lemon, rhubarb, grape, banana, apple, pineapple, mango, fig, cherry. cabbage, carrot, pea, bean, celery, potato, turnip, peppers, leek, corn, parsnip, mushroom, onion, kale, radish, spinach, lettuce, broccoli, yam, lentil.

Brainstorm (page 86)
1. Four wings 2. Ebony 3. Ken Doherty of Ireland 4. "…does not make a summer." 5. It was the first spacecraft to land on Mars, in March 1976. 6. Snowflakes have six sides. 7. 50 metres and 8 lanes 8. The Condor 9. Vitamin C 10. The hovercraft

What's the Difference? (page 91)

Hospital Health (page 94)
Across: 1. Ambulance 5. Theatre 7. Stethoscope 10. Operate 12. Recovered 13. Pulse
Down: 1. Heart 2. Antiseptic 3. Exercise 4. Switzerland 6. Thermometer 8. Saliva 9. Illness 11. Tendon

Brainstorm (page 95)
1. West to east 2. Michael Jordan 3. Victoria Falls 4. The hummingbird 5. Joan of Arc 6. In Wall Street 7. A lodge 8. Caves 9. Silver wedding anniversary 10. Red

Puzzle it Out (page 97)
Can You Draw This?

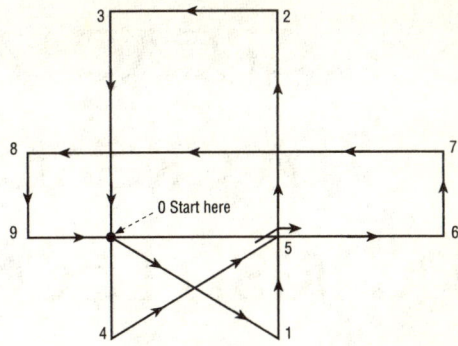

Total Brainteaser (page 97)

The Right Order (page 102)

```
P R O U D      O R D E R      F A B L E
R O P E S      F O R C E      L A I R S
I D E A L      F A I N T      O U T E R
N A N N Y      I N N E R      W A T E R
C H E S S      C A K E S      E V E N T
E L D E R      E A S E D      R A N G E

G A M E S      K I C K S      N A M E D
L E A R N      E A R L Y      U N I O N
O N I O N      T R A D E      M I S T Y
V I D E O      T E M P T      B A T H E
E X E R T      L U P I N      E V E N T
S I N C E      E A S E D      D E R B Y
```

Trick Your Friends (page 103)
3. The answer is "Flash in <u>the the</u> pan" because the other two were "Wind in <u>the the</u> Willows" and "Once in <u>a a</u> blue moon".

GREAT LAUGHS
A GREAT READ
THE IRISH LEGENDS SERIES

A GREAT NEW SERIES FROM BLACKWATER PRESS

The Gobán Saor has built a new house for a rich man. But what if the rich man tries to cheat him on the price? How can the Gobán Saor get his money then? Well, the wily builder knows the answer to that one... By the author of *The Yuckee Prince*.

The Scots Giant is coming to take Fionn's head! But what can Fionn do when Oonagh, his wife, won't let him fight? How can he save his head and avoid going into battle with the Scots Giant?

What is King Lory's secret? Why does he always wear a hood on his head? The widow's son is the only one who knows, but he has promised not to tell anybody and the secret is making him very ill!

Fionn and the Scots Giant and *The King's Secret* are by the best-selling author of *Return To Troy* and *Brainstorm*.

Three delightfully funny and uniquely retold well-loved tales.

£3.99 each